PHILIP OSBOURNE

THE DIARY OF PHIL THE
NerD

THE LIGHTS OF HOLLYWOOD

THE STORY OF A VERY SPECIAL KID
WHO BELIEVES IN FANTASY

ILLUSTRATIONS BY ROBERTA PROCACCI

I'm Phil, the nerd, the bookworm, the geek, the compulsive mathematician. If you are like me and sometimes people make fun of you, laugh it up. Who wrote the most famous bestsellers? The nerds. Who directed the biggest Hollywood blockbusters? The nerds. Who created the most advanced technology that can be only understood by its own creators? The nerds. So then, lift your heads up out of your books and smile to the world. Be proud to be a nerd like me. I'm Phil, Phil the Nerd to my friends... and I'm proud of it!

BEFORE I BEGIN...
LET ME INTRODUCE YOU TO MY FAMILY

Ellen is my sister.
She is a 9-year-old business genius.
You got it right: she dreams about having her own fashion company. Do you think it's normal to read financial newspapers at 9?
She is scary, believe me!
She is a little girl, but speaks just like a college graduate. She plans everything and, unlike me, looks after every detail.
She is determined and loves being our leader.
She is the youngest, but that doesn't keep her from making decisions for us all!
Don't ask me how she does it, but she manages to plan our days top to bottom. One more thing she loves is yelling at us: "Hurry up! It's almost tomorrow!"

Mom

Mom got famous when she designed a successful line of tongue-in-cheek t-shirts. Blogs and magazines say she's really cool. Her Facebook page reached 100,000 likes, and her t-shirts' quotes are among the most tweeted hashtags. You'll find everything about her on Pinterest.

Dad

He got fed up working as a manager and quit. He got himself a studio away from the city where he writes stories and essays about UFOs. Just to give you an idea of what Dad is like, listen to this: He was taking me to school and, as he parked the car, I asked him if he really believed aliens existed. He answered, "UFOs do exist. Aviation doesn't."

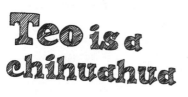

Teo is our little dog who doesn't bark, loves reading comics on his iPad, and uses Whatsapp even though he doesn't have fingers!

AND MY FRIENDS...
THE PING PONG THEORY

George

A hacker who looks like Chewbacca.

Big Mind Kill

She is gorgeous and a genius in mathematics. She can hypnotize anyone with a single look. She was my enemy before, but now she is part of my team: The Ping Pong Theory.

Nicholas

Nicholas is shy and hides his face under a paper bag.

To my two kids, without whom my fantasy would be a less beautiful place.
PHILIP OSBOURNE

Illustrations:
ROBERTA PROCACCI

FOR ABLAZE

Managing Editor
RICH YOUNG

Editor
KEVIN KETNER

Designer
RODOLFO MURAGUCHI

Publisher's Cataloging-in-Publication Data

Names: Osbourne, Philip, author.
Title: Diary of a nerd, vol. 2: the story of a special boy who believes in
fantasy (a lot) / written and illustrated by Philip Osbourne.
Description: "The Thousand Lights of Hollywood." — from cover. | Portland, OR: Ablaze Publishing, 2022.
| Summary: Phil, twelve, a self-professed nerd, along with the Geek Team, take a trip to Hollywood.
Identifiers: ISBN: 978-1-950912-29-2
Subjects: LCSH Friendship—Juvenile fiction. | Diaries—Juvenile fiction. | Hollywood (Los
Angeles, Calif.)—Juvenile fiction. | Humorous stories. | Graphic novels. | Comic books,
strips, etc. | CYAC: Friendship—Fiction. | Diaries—Fiction. | Hollywood (Los Angeles,
Calif.)—Fiction. | BISAC JUVENILE FICTION / Comics & Graphic Novels / General
Classification: LCC PZ7.7 .O766 2022 | DDC 741.5/973—dc23

10 9 8 7 6 5 4 3 2 1

BEFORE...

by Phil Dickens A.K.A. PHIL THE NERD

Yes, I'm a **NERD**. But, you shouldn't picture me as one of those kids who locks himself up in his room and stares at his computer all day. Of course, I spend time doing that (a lot of time), but if you asked me: "Hey, man, do you have a life?" I would never answer: "Where can I download it?" **I'M A NERD** who likes having fun and occasionally causing trouble. **I LOVE FENCING** (I'm an épée fencer), **I LOVE STAR WARS** (although the latest movies are even sadder than a clown kicked out of a circus) and sometimes I have strange visions, namely of **Darth Vader** or someone that looks like him who wants to give me all kinds of strange advice. Luckily, I have my amazing friends! They're the ones who bring me back to reality. **Nicholas**, **George** and **Big Mind Kill** are a big part of my life and so is

5

my sister **Ellen**, who's always helping
me solve any problems that come up.
All together, we go by the name of
THE PING PONG THEORY and
we take part in Mathematics competitions.
My heart beats for **BIG MIND KILL.**
I'm crazy about her. That's why I realized
something very important: I have to brush
my teeth everyday, so when she gets close
to me she won't wonder if I love onions.
For quite a while now, I've been waking
up in the morning thinking about her and
POKEMON. I'm still a nerd, so I tend to
mix up everything I'm passionate about!
What you're about to read is my new adventure,
the story of a young nerd who believes
in the power of imagination. As **Albert
Einstein** said: "Logic will get you from A
to B. Imagination will take you everywhere."
**LET THE DOOR OF YOUR
IMAGINATION OPEN
AND DISCOVER NEW
WORLDS WITH ME!**

CHAPTER ONE

Super Nerds & Super Lies

i WON'T TELL ANY MORE LiES.
OK, i KNOW, i JUST TOLD
ONE! WELL THEN, i WON'T
TELL THE TRUTH ANYMORE.
BEiNG HONEST iS EASY.

THE SUPER NERD
Something is wrong!
By Phil Dickens A.K.A PHIL THE NERD

Dear Diary,

imagine you're **BATMAN**.

Imagine you're that super cool guy with your

Batmobile in your **BATCAVE**, wearing your

Batsuit and fighting the most powerful

SUPER VILLAINS on Earth.

Just imagine you're him. Everybody admires

you and wants to hang out

with you. You're not afraid of anything and you always get what you want.

You are **BATMAN**, the Dark Knight. You're **BRUCE WAYNE**, the billionaire, one of the wealthiest and most powerful people in the whole world. Think about all the hi-tech equipment that **WAYNE ENTERPRISES** produces and it's all yours!

You're the coolest guy ever!

Can you imagine that?

Can you push your imagination to the limit and picture yourself engaged in an epic fight against the **JOKER**?

Will you be ready to repeat **BATMAN'S** most famous words: "Criminals are a superstitious, cowardly lot. So my disguise must be able to strike terror into their hearts. I must be a creature of the night, black, terrible..."?

Okay, then!

Dear Diary, I thought I was **BATMAN**, but when I woke up this morning, I felt a lot more like **TWEETY** Bird, locked in a cage, and with a "puddy tat a creepin' up on me."

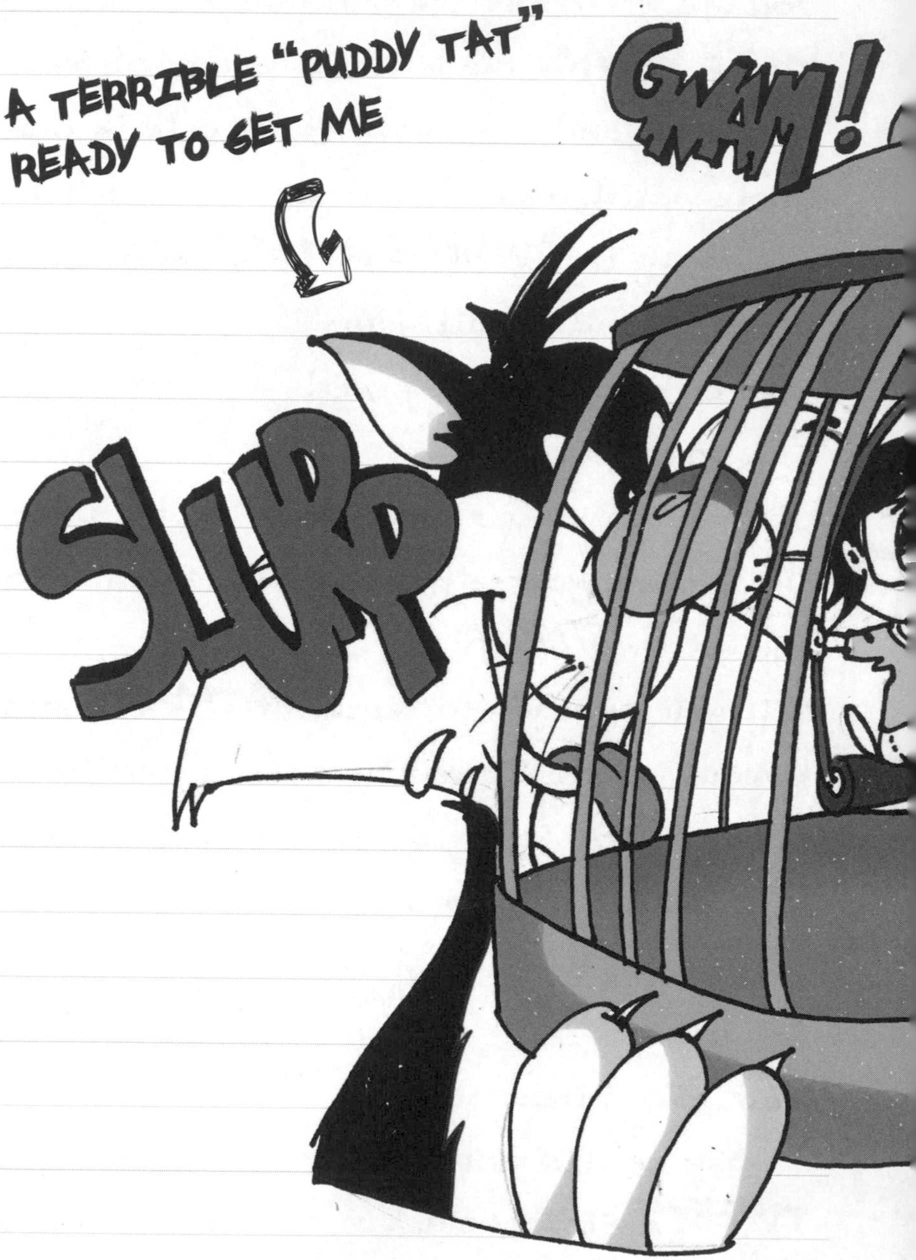
A TERRIBLE "PUDDY TAT"
READY TO GET ME
GWAM!
SLURP

I thought
I was Batman, but
I was more like
Tweety

PHIL, THE NERD

OH... OH...

I'M DEFINITELY NOT Batman, NOT TODAY ESPECIALLY, BECAUSE I WAS NOT ABLE TO GET MY USUAL A+ AT SCHOOL. I FEEL LIKE TWEETY BIRD BEING CHASED BY Sylvester The Cat.

11

October 7th

Everyone always expects the best of me and I always expect the best of myself. I should just relax a little, or at least try to, but I can't because I'm totally obsessed with my grades. In my mind, they're like green, sharp-toothed, little monsters, like the ones in the **ZOMBIE TSUNAMI** game. To me, grades are terrible creatures that are always chasing me.

In my nightmares, I'm running away from them while they shout: "Do you want a good grade? Let us hug you!"
Is that crazy?

It's hard to feel happy when everyone is always expecting you to get straight A's.
The only one who doesn't expect anything of me is Dad, because the only thing that he's concerned about is when the aliens are going to land on our planet.

Even his jokes are crazy. The other day he asked me: "Do you know why I haven't been able to park on the **MOON** today?" I was dreading the punchline, so I just shrugged. "Because today the Moon is full!" he shouted. He's a terrible comedian!

My fear of getting a bad grade gets much worse when I enter the classroom of **Mr. Gray**, the new Math teacher. He always looks at me with a frown. I don't know why, but he just doesn't like me. **WHY ELSE WOULD HE DRAW A PICTURE OF ME BEING CHASED BY A MUMMY?**

14

That's what I saw him doing while he was explaining Euclid's Theory to the class. No one believes me, but I know that he can't stand me, and every time he asks me a question in class I start shaking, and then even the most simple things get really confusing. Everything I say or do irritates him. I can't help but thinking that we look a

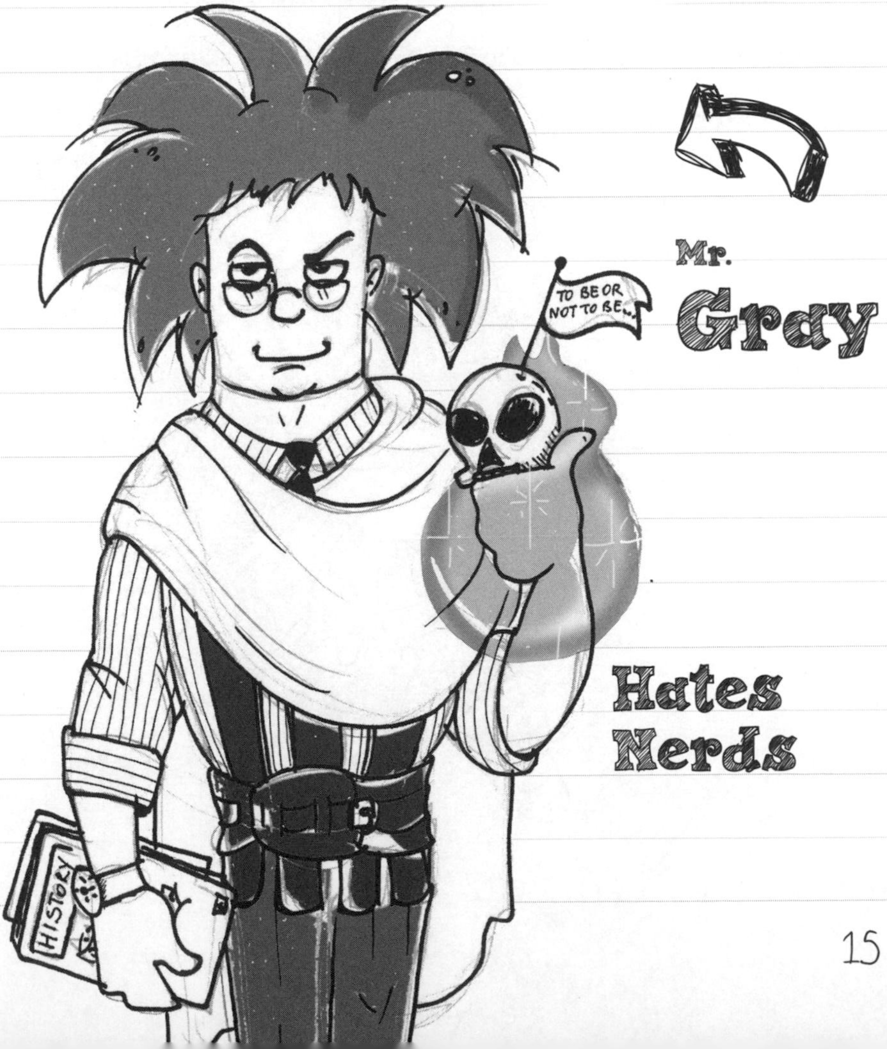
Mr. Gray
TO BE OR NOT TO BE...
Hates Nerds
HISTORY

little bit like **Bart Simpson** and **Sideshow Bob**.

MR. GRAY'S hair reminds me of a palm tree. And just like **BART'S** enemy, he loves showing off and reminding me that he is a very well-read, multilingual person who loves theater, opera, and...well, that he's a real culture snob. But trust me, under those phoney manners, he's just kind of a weird guy. He's like a cheerleader hippopotamus, or Hulk wearing a ballerina's tutu.

Why can't I
be a cheerleader, too?

Mr. Gray is a bully with no sense of humor. Last week he was scolding the class saying, "You kids are never going to make anything of your lives! **ESPECIALLY YOU NERDS**, who spend all your time playing videogames and reading comics!"

I knew he was talking about me.

For several days he had been taunting me and it wasn't just my imagination. But, unfortunately, I wasn't playing **MINECRAFT,** so I couldn't build castles and shelters, or dig deep underground in order to survive while I produced weapons and shields for protection against my enemies.

PHIL MINECRAFT NERD!!!

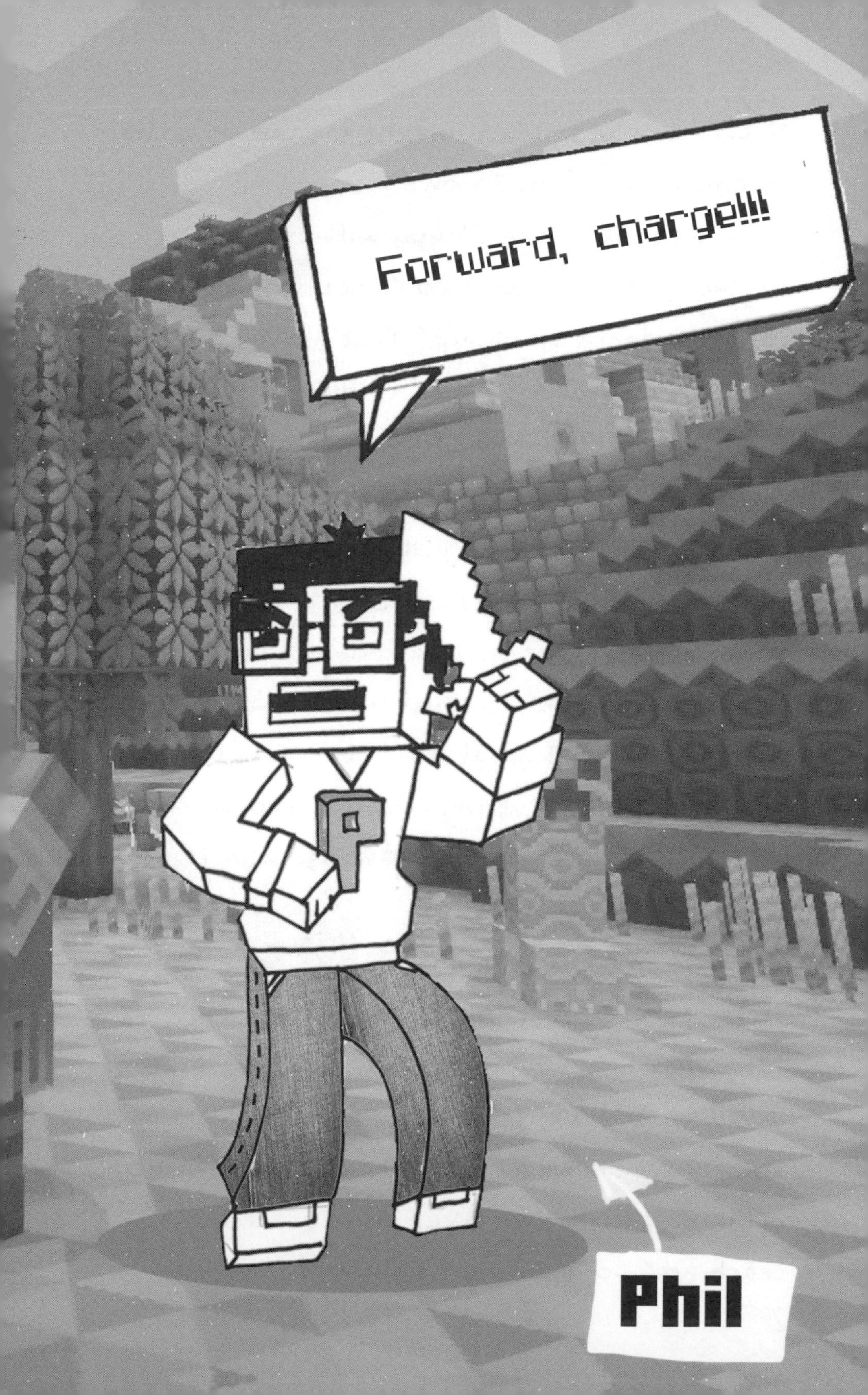
Forward, charge!!!
Phil

It was like he wanted to lure me out in order to break me down. I don't know why.

When he said, "None of you will ever make anything of your lives! Don't you wonder if you can even learn anything?" That's when my mind clouded over and I couldn't think straight. **Mr. Gray** then added, "And you, **PHIL**, my dear little **NERD**, put down your comics and video games, and just ask yourself if you are learning anything at all worthwhile!"

My mind went fuzzy. I felt like a volcano about to explode. I could barely contain my anger. I looked at him, stunned. I really work hard at my studies, and so does **NICHOLAS**. He's another **NERD** who is my friend and classmate.

Why was our teacher, **Mr. Gray**, being so nasty to us? I couldn't hold back my sarcasm when I replied. "I'm actually not wondering if I'm learning anything, because someone here who clearly hasn't ever learned a thing, decided to take up a career in teaching." Do you know Labyrinth, the old

20

movie starring **David Bowie?**
The main character was named Sarah, and the
first person she met was **HOGGLE**, an ugly
gnome who sprayed fairies with poison at
the entrance of the labyrinth. Well, Mr. Gray
looks like Hoggle, except taller and wider,
and he definitely didn't appreciate my insult.

So, he gave me a C, which is not a bad grade for most students, but is a terrible grade for me, since I'm used to getting an A+. He had succeeded in provoking me and I had lost my temper. I didn't feel like **BATMAN** anymore.

Goodbye Good Grades

From now on, I'll be nothing but an ordinary guy. No more adventures. I'm gonna miss you, Gotham. And you too, my beloved A+.

He had taken my batcave and my batmobile away from me and all of a sudden I had nothing but my beat up **PRIDE**.

October 8th

I needed to get back up on my **NERD** podium of having the best grades. But in order to do that, I managed to get myself into Big Trouble! I guess I just didn't want my friends to know I had gotten a C and wasn't so great after all.

DON'T YOU THINK THAT YOUR IMAGINATION HAS EXAGGERATED... JUST A LITTLE?

Big Mind Kill was so **BEAUTIFUL**, it was hard for me talk to her without sounding like an idiot. She had amazing eyes and she loved all the things I loved, too. She was **WONDER WOMAN** and **I WAS BATMAN**. We lived in the same world. She loved online role-playing games and she went crazy for Clash Royale, just like I did! She got lost in the whole **DR. OCTOPUS/ SPIDER-MAN** saga, and got furious when Han Solo died in **STAR WARS** VII. She had also tried to tell the internet how cool **HEROES** was and that **HEROES REBORN** was worth watching, too.

NERD TIME AGAINST STAR WARS VII

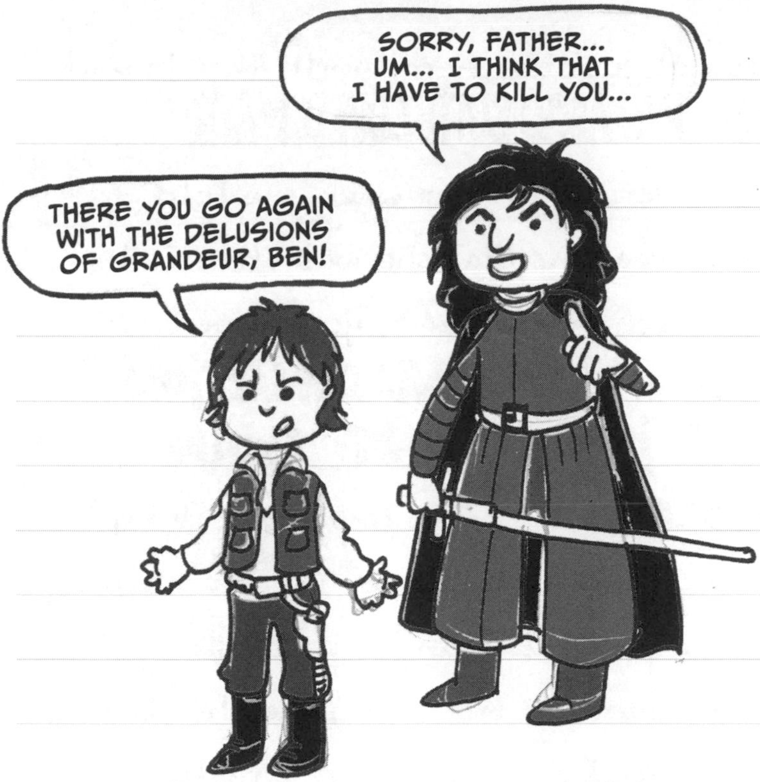
SORRY, FATHER... UM... I THINK THAT I HAVE TO KILL YOU...
THERE YOU GO AGAIN WITH THE DELUSIONS OF GRANDEUR, BEN!

Phil's fury

THERE ARE CERTAIN THINGS THAT A NERD CANNOT ENDURE!

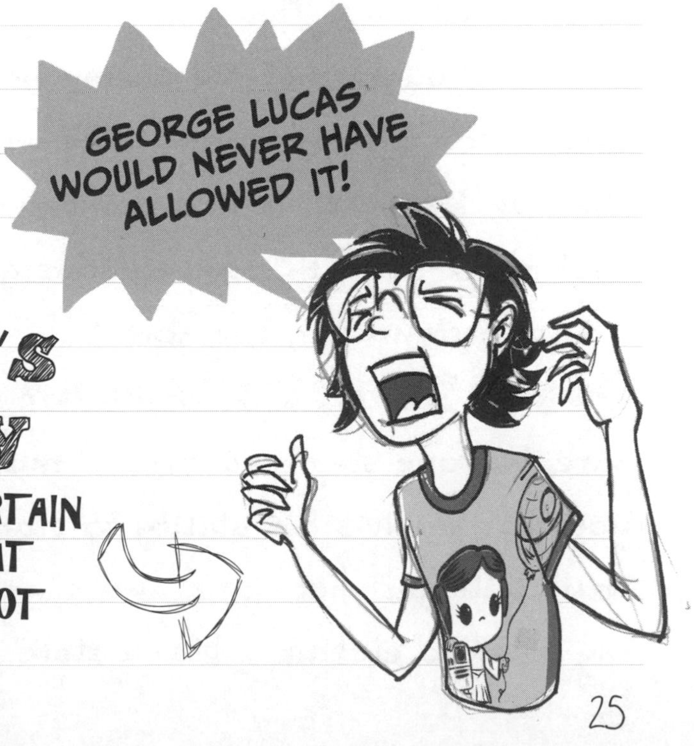
GEORGE LUCAS WOULD NEVER HAVE ALLOWED IT!

But it was not just our nerd world that bound us together. WE ALSO BOTH LOVED MATH. I really went crazy for her when she told me the three reasons that she was attracted to mathematics. "EINSTEIN, you know Albert Einstein, he said: IMAGINATION IS MORE IMPORTANT THAN KNOWLEDGE. Two: The important thing is to not stop questioning. Three: The search for truth is more precious than its possession. When I read those quotes I tried to understand what the reason behind them was, and I realized it was Mathematics. That's why I love it so much!" I never thought that my enemy would be the one person that I wanted to be with all the time. In the past, we had competed against each other in math competitions and I couldn't stand her, but now...

Do you think I'm in love?

Sure, but one step at a time. I must remind you that she has the ability to black out your mind with just her gaze, and I wouldn't want my mind to end up a blank slate.

26

I decided to confess my feelings for her, but when **BIG MIND KILL** told me that **NICHOLAS** and **GEORGE** were waiting for us in my sister **ELLEN'S** office, I decided to put off telling her for the moment. I had to devote my energies to something else: I wanted to hack into the school's computer and **change my grade from a C to an A**. That way my grade average wouldn't fall and everyone would still see me as the **SUPER NERD**.

SUPER PHIL

Super grades.
Super grade average.
Super liar.

BIG MIND KILL and I went to my sister's office...well, actually her bedroom that she had turned into a conference room. None of us knew what she wanted to tell us. **SHE LOOKED LIKE VICKY FROM THE FAIRLY ODD PARENTS.** Vicky was a greedy, sadistic, terrible babysitter. Only Ellen wasn't a babysitter, even though she did take care of our whole "**Ping Pong Theory**" team. **NICHOLAS** was already sitting there with his paper bag over his head, and **GEORGE** was taking notes on his computer so that he could protest against anything my sister might say. **ELLEN** and my two friends were scared of **BIG MIND KILL**, not because she dressed like a goth-girl, but because of her hypnotic gaze. As she entered the office, she showed off her brightest, toothpaste-ad-like smile to everyone.

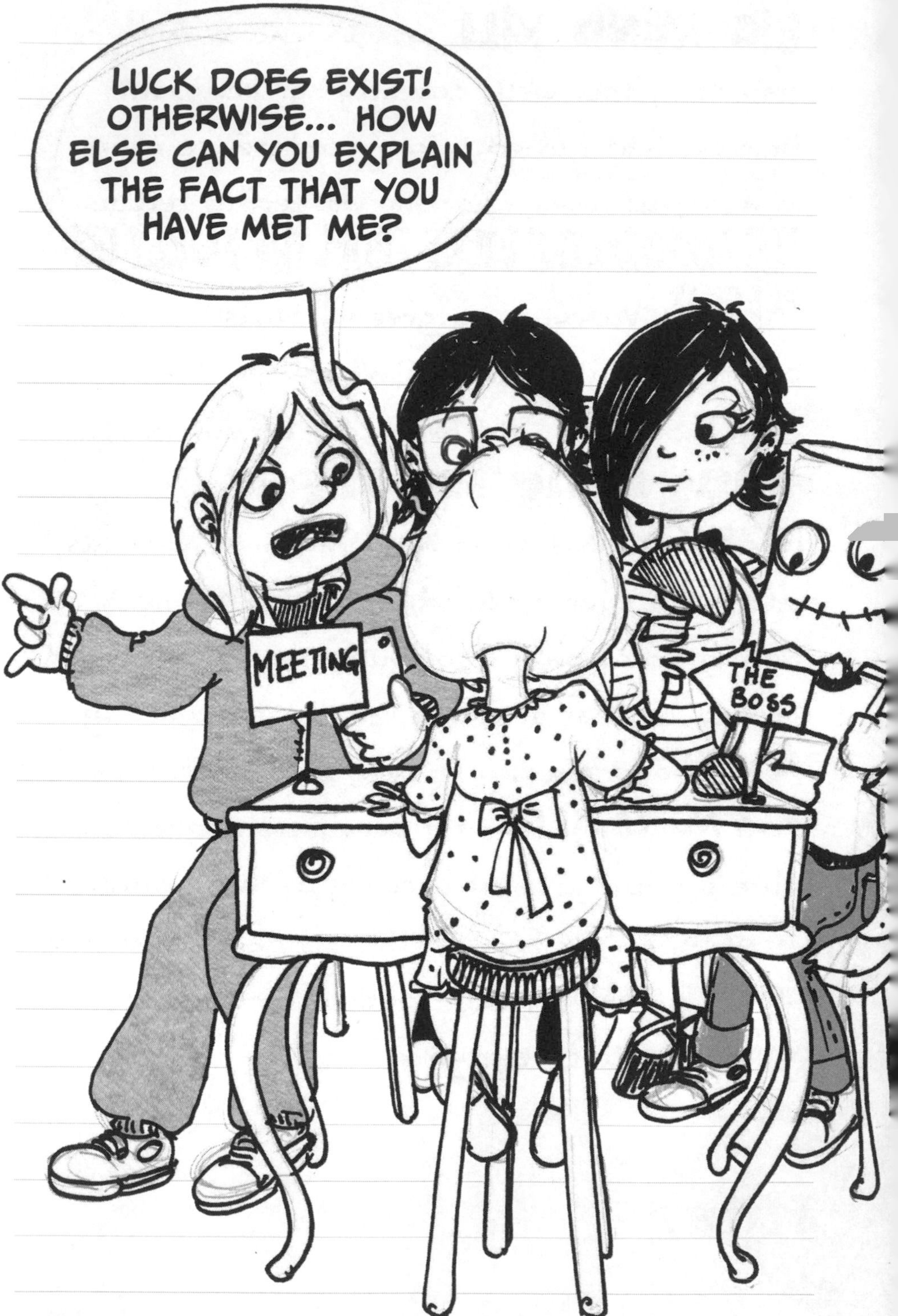
LUCK DOES EXIST! OTHERWISE... HOW ELSE CAN YOU EXPLAIN THE FACT THAT YOU HAVE MET ME?
MEETING
THE BOSS

"**BiG MiND KiLL**, now that you are a member of our team, you should know that I am the coach! And **I LOVE DEMOCRACY ABOUT AS MUCH AS A DOG LOVES A CAT**. So you see, dear, I make all the decisions around here!" **ELLEN** announced in order to clear up any misunderstandings.

BIG MIND KILL just smiled.

She realized that **ELLEN** might be small, but she was really shrewd.

She decided to let my little sister play out her boss role to avoid disrupting the balance of power on our team.

"Guys, I have a surprise for you!" **ELLEN** continued.

"Please, don't ask us to clean up your room," **NICHOLAS** said from under the paper bag.

GEORGE said, "Generally, what you call surprises are what the rest of us call problems."

"Please, let her explain," **BIG MIND KILL** said.

ELLEN SMILED and said: "Thank you for your female solidarity, **BIG MIND KILL**.

Boys generally don't realize that the beginning of a new day for a boy is the end of a day for us girls. We're always one step ahead of them.

Anyway, I have summoned you here today to talk to you about the TV show, '**AMERICA LOVES TALENT**.'"

Our eyes lit up.

~~**AMERICA LOVES TALENT**~~ was the most popular show on television, and there were hundreds of Facebook pages about the show's contestants. All of them were really cool, clever people, but completely crazy. It was a show that everyone liked because teams of contestants competed in tests of intelligence and logic, and the participants were oddball people with ridiculous names. I remember a team from Ohio called **THE PARASITES** who dressed up as mushrooms. They actually defeated **THE BLOTCHIES**, a bunch of ex mathematics professors from Texas with faces full of pimples.

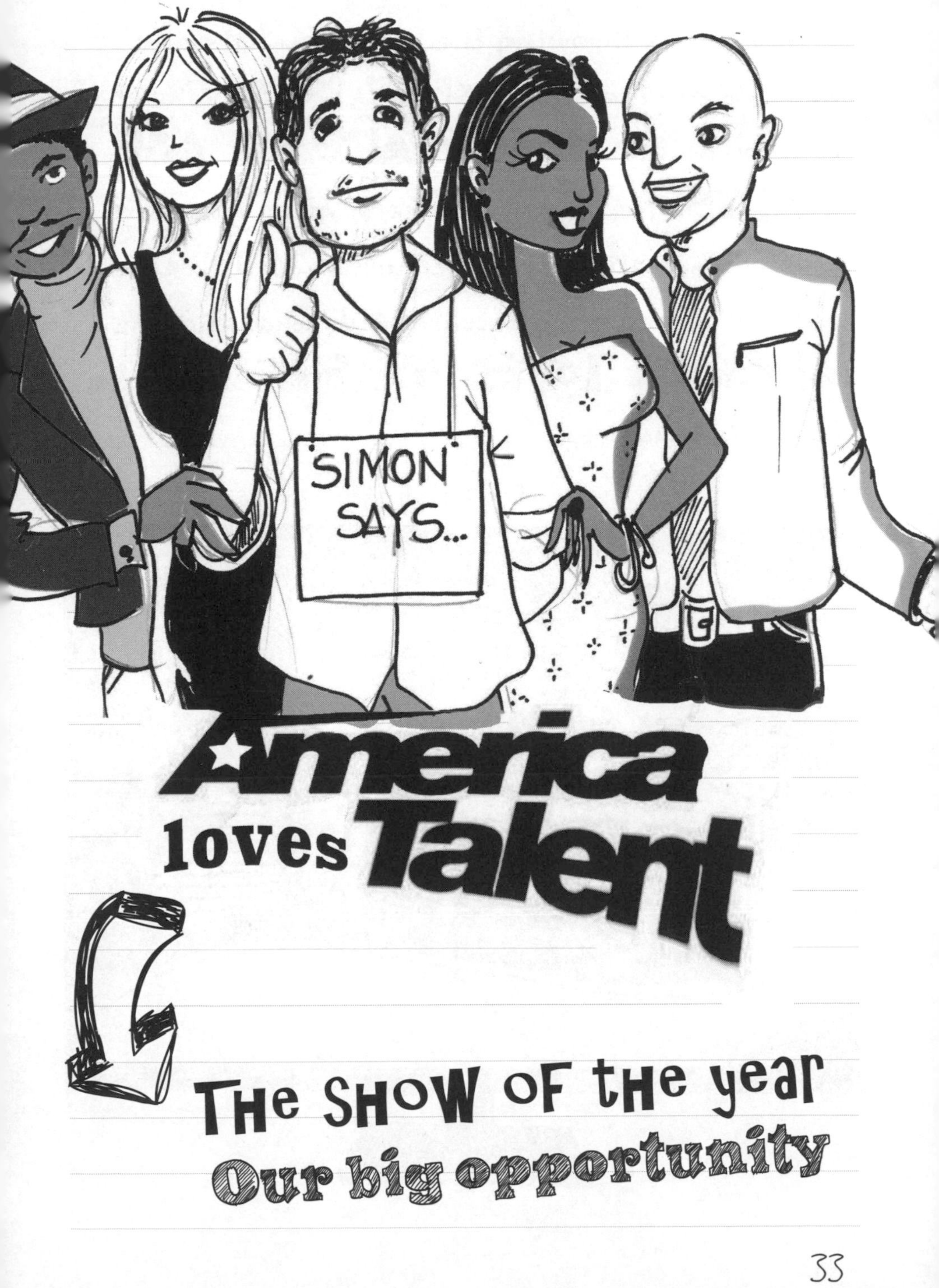
SIMON SAYS...

America loves Talent

The SHOW OF the year

Our big opportunity

They were so boring, they couldn't stop arguing and throwing their cowboy hats at each other. The show's **GRAND PRIZE** is a lot of money, and **THERE ARE NO AGE LIMITS**. That's why teachers, mad scientists, and mathematicians gone nuts waited in line for a chance to participate. But, what did the **AMERICA LOVES TALENT** show have to do with us?

"Is this another competition for us to face?" I asked, worriedly.

"THE SCHOOL IS SUCH A LIMITED ENVIRONMENT FOR OUR GREAT ABILITIES," ELLEN answered, determinedly. "We have a new member now, quite a valuable one indeed. If we play our cards right, we can win this thing." BIG MIND KILL smiled. She was happy that ELLEN was PUTTING HER TRUST IN THE OTHER GIRL ON OUR TEAM.

"Despite GEORGE'S presence," ELLEN continued, "we're a very talented team and we could defeat adults, too, if we really focus on our scientific and mathematics skills."

"Despite having a coach like Ellen," GEORGE replied sarcastically, "whose speaking abilities surpass her limited thinking skills, I too think we could win this thing." NICHOLAS was happy about it all. He was used to ELLEN and GEORGE'S bickering, and by now he didn't even notice them. He was a NEW YORK METS fan who loved competition,

35

and he asked: "Do they accept contestants who wear paper bags over their heads?"

BIG MIND KILL was amazed by all of this and sounded like a grown-up when she asked, "Don't you think there could be teams that are better prepared than us, like some university students or teachers? And what makes you think that **AMERICA LOVES TALENT** would accept us? It's a TV show after all, and maybe we're not as weird and unique as they would want us to be!"

ELLEN climbed up on her desk.

She was going to put on her big show of being the boss. She frowned and said very seriously, "**LOOK AT YOURSELVES!**"

She pointed her finger at us and continued. "What group would have a super charming 9-year-old girl for its boss, **SOMEONE WHOSE MANAGERIAL SKILLS ARE ALMOST UNPRECEDENTED ON THE PLANET EARTH?**

Now you can understand why they **ACCEPTED** US as soon as I sent them the picture of our team.

36

NICHOLAS GEORGE

BURP

GEORGE FINDS IT EASIER TO SMILE WHEN HE IS WITH US.

GEORGE LOOKS LIKE THE LESS COOL BROTHER OF CHEWBACCA, BUT CAN HE EVEN LOOK "NORMAL" FOR A FEW MOMENTS WHILE HE TRIES TO HACK INTO YOUTUBE?

BIG MIND KILL

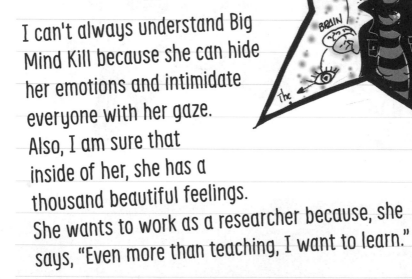

I can't always understand Big Mind Kill because she can hide her emotions and intimidate everyone with her gaze. Also, I am sure that inside of her, she has a thousand beautiful feelings.

She wants to work as a researcher because, she says, "Even more than teaching, I want to learn."

PHIL, THE NERD

Am I a superhero? I see everything like it was in a comic book or in a TV series. Sometimes I feel like Flash, and think about what it would be like to go so fast that I would always be the first one to arrive everywhere. I don't like to lose and I don't accept defeat, because I'm afraid of disappointing my parents and my teachers. They always expect the best from me!

39

It's official: THE PING PONG THEORY are going to be on **AMERICA LOVES TALENT**. If someone wins, someone else loses... and we don't intend to be that 'someone else,'" said **ELLEN**.

ELLEN, THE BOSS

My sister loves to organize and give orders. Her first word wasn't "mama" or "dada," but "I." She doesn't mean to micro-manage everything, she just does it because it comes natural to her.

In her defense, she says: "There are kids who like to follow, and I just want to make them happy!"

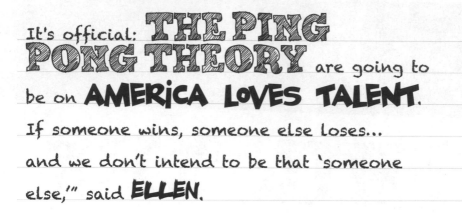

"Where will the competition be held?" asked **NICHOLAS**.

"At their studios in Hollywood," **ELLEN** answered calmly.

Were we really going to California? All of us together?

"Yes, we are going to Hollywood... but we'll first have to convince our parents, of course," said our mini-boss.

HOLLYWOOD is where all the movies and TV series that I love are shot! Maybe we would get to see some sets and meet some actors!

SUPER MEGA WOW!!!!

For a moment, I pictured myself having lunch with **GEORGE LUCAS**, while he told me some **STAR WARS** secrets.

October 9th

Dear Diary,

You should already know by now that I have a real talent for getting into trouble.

The bad grade that **Mr. Gray** gave me was completely unfair. I absolutely didn't deserve it. And it was very clear that he hated me. So, I had to do something. In **BIG HERO 6**, **BAYMAX** was a sweet, comforting robot nurse, but when he got upset, he went down to the street and decided **TO FIGHT CRIME**. The healthcare-chip in his body wouldn't allow him to hurt anyone, but when it was taken out, leaving only the fighting-chip, **BAYMAX** would go **BERSERK**. His eyes turned red and he became a killing machine that wouldn't stop until he reached his target. That's how I feel now. I switched into `BERSERK-MODE` and was determined that **Mr. Gray** had to give me the grade **I DESERVED**.

The bell had just rung and everybody was leaving school... except for me.

A few minutes earlier, just before the end of class, I had to endure another one of **Mr. Gray's** rants about how useless and stupid **NERDS** are. "The problem with some of these nerds is how presumptuous they are. They see themselves as superheroes just because they read **MARVEL** or **DC COMICS**. They think they're immortal because they watch **The Walking Dead**. Dear nerds, and I'm talking to you, Nicholas and **MR. PHIL DICKENS**, you are not superheroes. Sometimes life might take you by surprise," he said with an evil smile. It really sounded like a threat, but I didn't say anything because I didn't want to get into more trouble with him. He was just waiting for me to give an angry reply so that he would have a reason to expel me from school.

44

I had to do something quick in order to keep my grade point average up. Why did **Mr. Gray** want to humiliate us nerds?

I broke into the school's computer room. I HAD VERY LITTLE TIME TO LOG ONTO THE SCHOOL'S SERVER AND UNDO THE INJUSTICE THAT I HAD SUFFERED.

I turned on the computer and connected to the server, and thanks to an app that allowed me to check all the passwords **Mr. Gray** had been provided with, I hacked into his account.

Change the grade from 'C' to 'A'

CHANGE THE GRADE... 10

LOADING

10 8

The perfect internet pirate

The one-eyed parrot of the perfect internet pirate

Once I was in, I could access the official **Register of Grades**. I had never done anything like that in my whole life, but that awful man deserved it. In just a few seconds, my C had been turned into an A+.

SUDDENLY I HEARD A NOISE, AND I ALMOST SCREAMED IN FEAR. I scanned the whole room like a drone and, finally, realized there was no one there. Thank goodness!

If someone had seen me, I **WOULD HAVE BEEN EXPELLED** and my academic career would have been buried underground with the creatures from **TREMORS**.

When I left school, I was really happy because I had restored my report card to the grades that I deserved.

Now I just needed to understand why **Mr. Gray** hated **NERDS** so much.

NERD TIME:
What is TREMORS?

Have you ever heard of **Tremors**? Of course not! I can talk about it because, as a true nerd, I have watched all the fantasy and sci-fi films from the 1980s and '90s. In Tremors, there are some strange, gigantic creatures called "Graboids" that look like huge worms and live under the desert. They are blind, but have super hearing. They are attracted to the vibrations on the surface and come up to eat – not just cows and other animals, but also humans!

WE DON'T ONLY EAT ANIMALS...

DID THAT LOOK LIKE A "COW" THING TO YOU?!!??

October 10th

It was Sunday, so I wanted to sleep in and try
to forget about what I had done.
I couldn't even imagine what kind of
punishment I would get if my parents ever
found out that I had changed my grades.
Then I realized that my mother was trying to
pull me out of bed.
"Wake up! **BIG MIND KILL** is in the living
room and she looks pretty upset," Mom said
forcefully. For a moment I was afraid that
the school had caught on to what I had done.
I got up quickly, and with my **PUNISHER**
t-shirt on, I went to see her
immediately. "What's going on?"
I asked nervously.

(Marvel vigilante
hero created by
Gerry Conway,
John Romita Sr.
and Ross Andru.)

She was as pale as a zombie. Whatever
had happened that made her come to my
house on a Sunday morning must be a **BIG**
PROBLEM.
Big Mind Kill switched on her computer.
She opened a **Facebook** page and showed it

48

to me. It was the profile of a guy who called himself **SKELETOR**. I burst out laughing like I was watching a new episode of **ADVENTURE TIME**.

SKELETOR

"What kind of person would call himself **SKELETOR**? Don't tell me he's into the He-Man cartoons? It was a really terrible show from the 1980s. At least that's what my father says, and he was also a nerd!" I said.

"He calls himself Skeletor because he is really treacherous and everyone is afraid of him," **BIG MIND KILL** said. "And he is one of the most brutal hackers, he's ruthless.

He's 17-years-old, completely cold-blooded, and a **REAL GENIUS**.

Skeletor is mathematics come to life! I've never seen him with his eyes off his computer or his math books!

HE DOESN'T GET ALONG WITH ANYONE AND HE SPENDS ALL HIS TIME CREATING TERRIBLE COMPUTER VIRUSES!" she said.

"Well, what does this have to do with us?"

"Read his last post!" yelled **BIG MIND KILL**.

¡ WAS SPEECHLESS!

Mr. Gray was going to be coach of The Evil Avengers, a super team he

I'm happy to announce to you that Mr. Gray has just recruited me to the Evil Avengers Team and that we are going to participate in **AMERICA LOVES TALENT**. I can't wait to meet the three other members who will join us to fight and triumph and win the Grand Prize!

had created to fight against **THE PiNG PONG THEORY!** Now it was clear: **Mr. Gray hated me and the Nerds,** and that made me really scared!

Mr. Gray was a true evil genius. He anticipated all of his enemies' moves- And now I knew that I was one of them!

MY DEAR WILE E., IF YOU HAD ONLY CALLED ME EARLIER, JUST THINK OF ALL THE TROUBLE YOU COULD HAVE SAVED YOURSELF.

GOSH

Phil's Diary

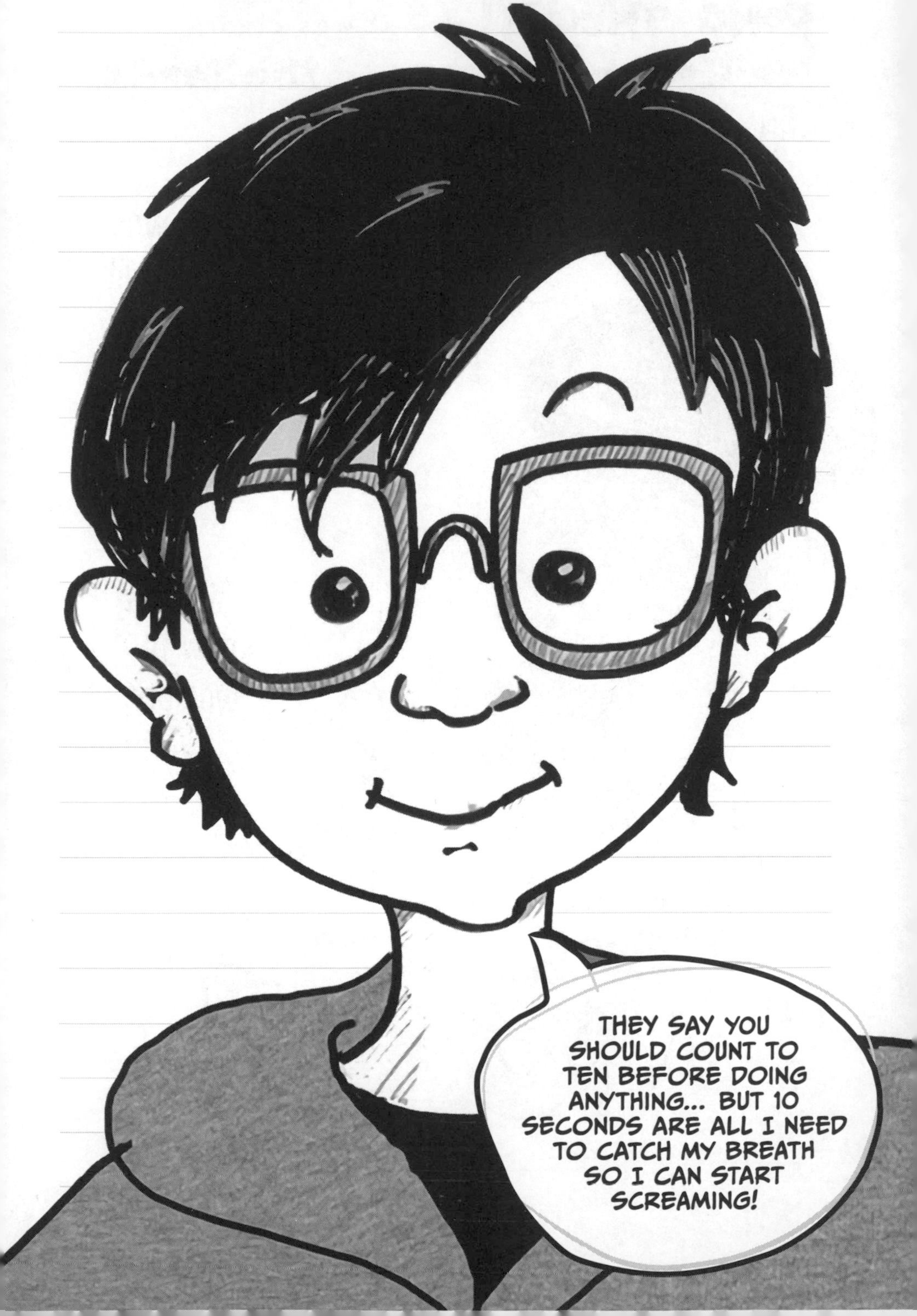
THEY SAY YOU SHOULD COUNT TO TEN BEFORE DOING ANYTHING... BUT 10 SECONDS ARE ALL I NEED TO CATCH MY BREATH SO I CAN START SCREAMING!

CHAPTER TWO

Do not go into those studios

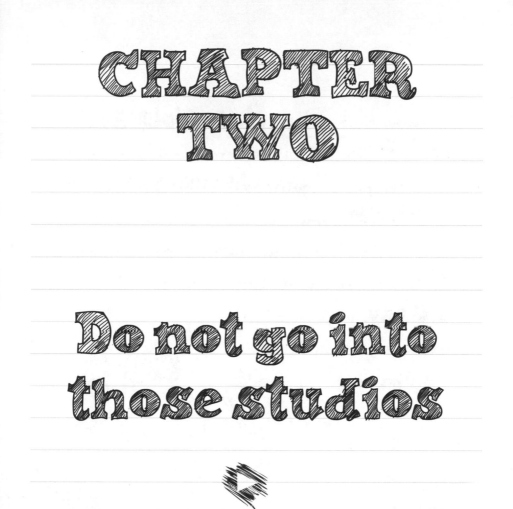

OK, i WAS WRONG... BUT
WHEN i'M 80 YEARS OLD,
i'LL PROBABLY HAVE LEARNED
EVERYTHING ABOUT LIFE.
THE PROBLEM WILL BE
REMEMBERING iT!

You know that movie, **NOW YOU SEE ME 2?** It's the one where magicians and mentalists fight against **ARTHUR TRESSLER'S** son, **WALTER**, who's taking revenge on the Four Horsemen after his father was defeated. Well, that's what I wanted to do to **Mr. Gray**. His hatred for nerds was finally out in the open and it made me furious, like the time Mom had called me in the middle of a duel in **Clash Royale** and it caused me to go back to the **ARENA**.

For a moment, I thought that my

54

stomach had turned into a centrifuge, because it felt like all my anger was rumbling in it. "WAKE UP!" **BIG MIND KILL** yelled to me as we were about to board our flight to **LA**. I was **SCARED** and angry, and I hadn't realized that now it was time to **go with my friends and family to Hollywood**.

My dad, in his usual daze, had been
STOPPED AT THE AIRPORT METAL DETECTOR.
He had set off all the alarms and a special anti-terrorism team tackled him and threw him to the floor. **MOM**, like all the other adults who were watching, stared at him and I could tell what she was thinking: **"I knew there was something wrong with my husband!"**

As soon as he saw my father on the floor with a rifle to his head, **GEORGE**, without his usual

My father carried a large stuffed toy of Alf. Alf is the main character of a sitcom that was broadcast by NBC from 1986 to 1990.

56

sarcasm, said: "Did your dad bring one of his aliens in with him?"

It wasn't anything to laugh at, because my friend was right.

THE POLICE QUESTIONED MY OLD MAN, asking why an adult would want to bring aboard the airplane a big stuffed toy of Alf (the alien main character of a 1980s sitcom). Without thinking, my father said: "BECAUSE ALIENS ARE AMONG US AND THEY ARE GOOD."

Talking with my dad is like riding downhill on a bicycle without brakes. It is impossible to stop or control him.

THE POLICE THOUGHT HE WAS COMPLETELY CRAZY and had thrown him to the ground. Since he was afraid they'd take Alf away from him, he yelled at the agent, which just made things worse.

"Don't open him up! He's on our side, he's good!"

He obviously REALLY LOVED ALF.

My dad has never realized that we live in a world of rules.

T-SHIRT
MADE BY
MOM

GOOD TO THOSE WHO ARE GOOD

HIS SIGHTS HAVE ALWAYS BEEN SET HIGH ABOVE THE EARTH,

in search of other worlds and the spaceships that would make him happy.

Perhaps he is not used to facing reality.

HE IS A MAN WHO IS DIFFICULT TO UNDERSTAND, but that's what makes him so adorable.

How he feels about **aliens** is how I feel about mathematics.

My mom was amused and scared at the same time. She knew that **LENNY** was like a game: sometimes he went to **GAME OVER** and other times he would take us up to the "next level."

MARILYN, aka my mom, in order to calm the police and keep my friends' parents from panicking, approached the **Head of Security** with one of her famous t-shirts. **THE OFFICER** looked like **ADAM SANDLER**, the actor from **Pixels** and **Grown Ups**, except he had a gold tooth. He seemed angry at first, but when he saw **MOM** with the t-shirt he calmed down. **"GOOD? WHO'S HE GOOD WITH?"** He asked, quoting the t-shirt slogan. The man looked at my dad and realized that he had misunderstood him. **"GOOD TO THOSE WHO ARE GOOD."** "Is he your husband?" **THE OFFICER** asked. "Yes, check out the stuffed toy he brought with him, he'd never hurt a fly. He loves aliens, especially the sitcoms and movies where they are portrayed as friendly, and he thinks that we shouldn't be afraid of them." My mother explained.

The **officer** took the alien and passed it through the metal detector.

When he realized it was nothing but an **Alf** stuffed toy, he apologized for the misunderstanding. He explained that the security protocols are necessary for our safety. Dad took his alien back and said: "**WAR OF THE WORLDS**, that movie with **TOM CRUISE** where the aliens arrive and attack us, really sucks!

Long live Alf!"

My friends' parents burst out laughing, and it certainly wasn't easy to explain to them later that the very same man who'd almost been arrested for **LOOKING LIKE A MAD MAN** was also the author who won the "**BEST ALIEN NOVEL AWARD**."

October 20th

In **HOLLYWOOD**, we were in a hotel where we had two connecting rooms. **I shared one room with my sister** and my parents were in the room next door, sleeping like logs. Dad wore his **IRON GIANT** pajamas (his favorite cartoon) and Mom wore one of her t-shirts that portrayed us all dressed up as the **FANTASTIC FOUR.** Our family's really weird!

ELLEN returned to our room to study the team that we would have to compete against on the **show.**

"**PHIL**, I want to analyze the **EVIL AVENGERS** and understand their weaknesses. We all have a weak spot and, usually, I'm one of them for our competitors!" She said with her usual adult attitude, even if she was only 9-years old.

"I'm **WORRIED**," I replied. "We're going to be on **AMERICA LOVES TALENT** and we'll have to fight for the title.

My parents were sleeping. Dad used to tell me that in his dreams humans are in black and white and aliens are in color. His Iron Giant pajamas are not what you'd call suitable for a man of his age, but he couldn't care less. He just wants to be happy with us and his "aliens."

It won't be as easy as the math tournament."

"You have to trust me. I am the wheels of your bicycle and I promise I'll get you there."

I LAID DOWN ON MY BED AND MY SISTER TOOK OUT HER MACBOOK AND HER PORTABLE PRINTER. She started doing her research and, after a while, she came to me with some printed pages.

"Now we know who your dear **Mr. Gray** has recruited to fight against us!" She was proud of herself.

I grabbed the first file.

"This one's called **MORTIMER**, AKA **THE WALKING DEAD**. He is 26-years-old, from Pasadena, and is said to be a real zombie. He never steps outside his house, not even to go grocery shopping. He only communicates by **TWITTER** and has never even exceeded the **280 CHARACTER** limit. He doesn't like speaking to other people much.

When he was 6-years-old, he amazed the whole world by solving the Matiyasevich Theorem in 3 minutes.

According to Wikipedia, he has also invented a **NEW VIRUS** capable of making you grow a third eye in the middle of your forehead. **BUT, THIS HASN'T BEEN CONFIRMED.**"

That **MORTIMER** was one creepy guy. Maybe it'd be better not to know anything about his teammates!

"You're **DYING** to know about the rest of the team, aren't you?" My sister asked. She actually wanted to **SCARE ME** more than inform me.

"The second profile is for **MISS SCREAM.**

She is 23-years-old and likes to wear the **SCREAM** mask from the TV series and the **WES CRAVEN** movie. She lives in **SALT LAKE CITY** and there are all sorts of stories about her on the **INTERNET,**" she continued.

64

Mortimer

THE EVIL AVENGERS

Many things are said about him... He is called The Walking Dead because he loves horror movies and always identifies with the Villain! He hates everyone, including himself, sometimes.

"I've read about how she managed to find the access code to get into a **Las Vegas** casino.

FILE:

NAME: Mortimer

NICKNAME: The Walking Dead

MAIN FEATURES: self-secluded loner, twitter addict, math genius

Definitely... Totally dangerous!

She'd **also been hired by the US government** to **TRY TO BREAK THROUGH THEIR SECURITY,** which she accomplished in less than 6 hours. Afterwards, however, she POSTED EVERYTHING ONLINE, including top secret documents. **SHE LOVES CREATING CHAOS.**"

We were the least **dangerous** people on the face of the **EARTH**. **Nicholas** and **George** could, at most, be able to scare a hill of ants. And as for me, I could only put my faith in **BIG MIND KILL'S** brain power.

FILE:

NAME: Miss Scream

FEATURES: Wears the Scream mask, famous hacker, she hates everything and everyone.

26-years-old

Definitely...Better to stay away from her!

"Before you go to bed, it's important for you to know who the last member of their team is. He's called **VENOM SLIM**.

Miss Scream

THe EViL Avengers

She never takes off that mask. It was inspired by the Wes Craven movie. No one can remember her face and no pictures are available online.

He looks exactly like **Venom**, **Spider-man's** nemesis, but he's more slender. He's 50-years-old and made a fortune on Wall Street. He's **SUPER RICH** and loves intimidating anyone that he thinks is **INTELLIGENT**. **HE ALWAYS WEARS A HORRIBLE SYMBIOTE ALIEN MASK.** He also **HATES** the sound of bells because of a childhood trauma: when he was a kid his friends stole his lunchbox close to a church and the bells were tolling. He **HATES** teenagers, and **LOVES TRIPPING ELDERLY PEOPLE.**"

They were all grown ups and really terrible! How could we ever beat them?

Their coach was my teacher, and they were all high school graduates with more knowledge than us. It was like daring **MESSI** to a free kick challenge. We were more likely to find a child taking the **LOCH NESS MONSTER** out for a walk on a leash than to win **AMERICA LOVES TALENT**.

THe EViL AveNgers
Venom Slim

Still October 20th

When you are **SCARED**, the night seems to never end. For me, the minutes passed by like hours... AND THE HOURS SEEMED LIKE MONTHS.

70

The night was like a funhouse mirror and made my thoughts weird and **INDECIPHERABLE. THE MOON WAS A PAINTER WHO ONLY KNEW THE COLOR GRAY.**

I was **afraid** that I would be humiliated on TV in front of millions of people. The **AMERICA LOVES TALENT** judges were not what you'd call friendly.

David Hasspig, who was famous in the '80s when he starred in that awful **SUPERSPACECAR TV** series, always made

fun of the contestants. **HE WAS THE WORST JUDGE** ever and, even though he knew nothing about Math, **HE STILL JUDGED THE TALENT OF SCIENTISTS** and mathematicians who competed in the show. He was really mean and he often posted the humiliated faces of the contestants on his **Instagram** page.

He seems to only be happy when other people are sad.

I could already imagine him taking a selfie with me crying in front of the **EVIL AVENGERS**. I was totally **stressed**, but I had to sleep, otherwise I would never make it through the competition. I tried counting sheep jumping a fence, but I still couldn't make it to the **WORLD OF DREAMS.** So I thought it'd be funnier to picture **POKEMON** jumping the fence. That's the **NERD'S** way to fall asleep. The average guy counts sheep, a nerd counts **POKEMON!**

Dear Diary, I normally don't dream about the characters who populate **comics, TV series** or **movies**. Yeah, well, I used to dream about **DARTH VADER**, but that wasn't really a dream, more like a vision. **HE WAS KIND OF LIKE A MENTOR TO ME**, advising me on what to do, and sometimes would even **APPEAR TO ME DURING THE DAY**.

YOU DON'T HA

YOU MUSTN'T SLEEP!

During the night of October 20th, I wished that
I could talk to **DARTH VADER**.

Maybe **he could have given me** some advice to cheer me up a little.

But instead, that night I was visited by a strange being that I couldn't ever have imagined.

Come on, try to guess what it was... It wasn't a **GORILLA**.

So it wasn't **KING KONG**.

It wasn't a monkey.

So it wasn't **CAESAR** from **Planet of the Apes**.

It wasn't a superhero fool.

So, **DEADPOOL** didn't show up.

Okay, I'm not going to keep you guessing! It was an **ALIEN!**

But not one like that lazy, centuries-old couch potato extraterrestrial from **Area 51** that **STAN** from **AMERICAN DAD** took home with him!

It was something much cooler!

It was **E.T.** Yes, him... or at least an alien that looked like the one from that famous film directed by **STEVEN SPIELBERG**.

He reached out his long 3-fingered hand to my iPhone and said to me:

"**E.T.** phone home!"

I thought the call would be very expensive so I asked if he could use someone else's phone. He started to laugh and said to me: "**Very funny!**"

Man, here I was with **E.T.**, the iconic extraterrestrial, and the only thing I could think of to say to him was don't use my iPhone.

"**LOOK ME IN THE EYES, BOY!**" the alien scolded me, angrily. I had remembered him as being very nice and kind.

"**FIND YOUR SPACESHIP HOME AND ALSO THE BALANCE OF THE VICTORY,**"

he said. What did he mean by that?
Was he talking about me getting into the school records and changing my grades?

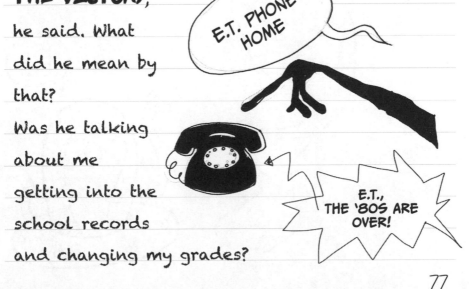

E.T. PHONE HOME

E.T., THE '80S ARE OVER!

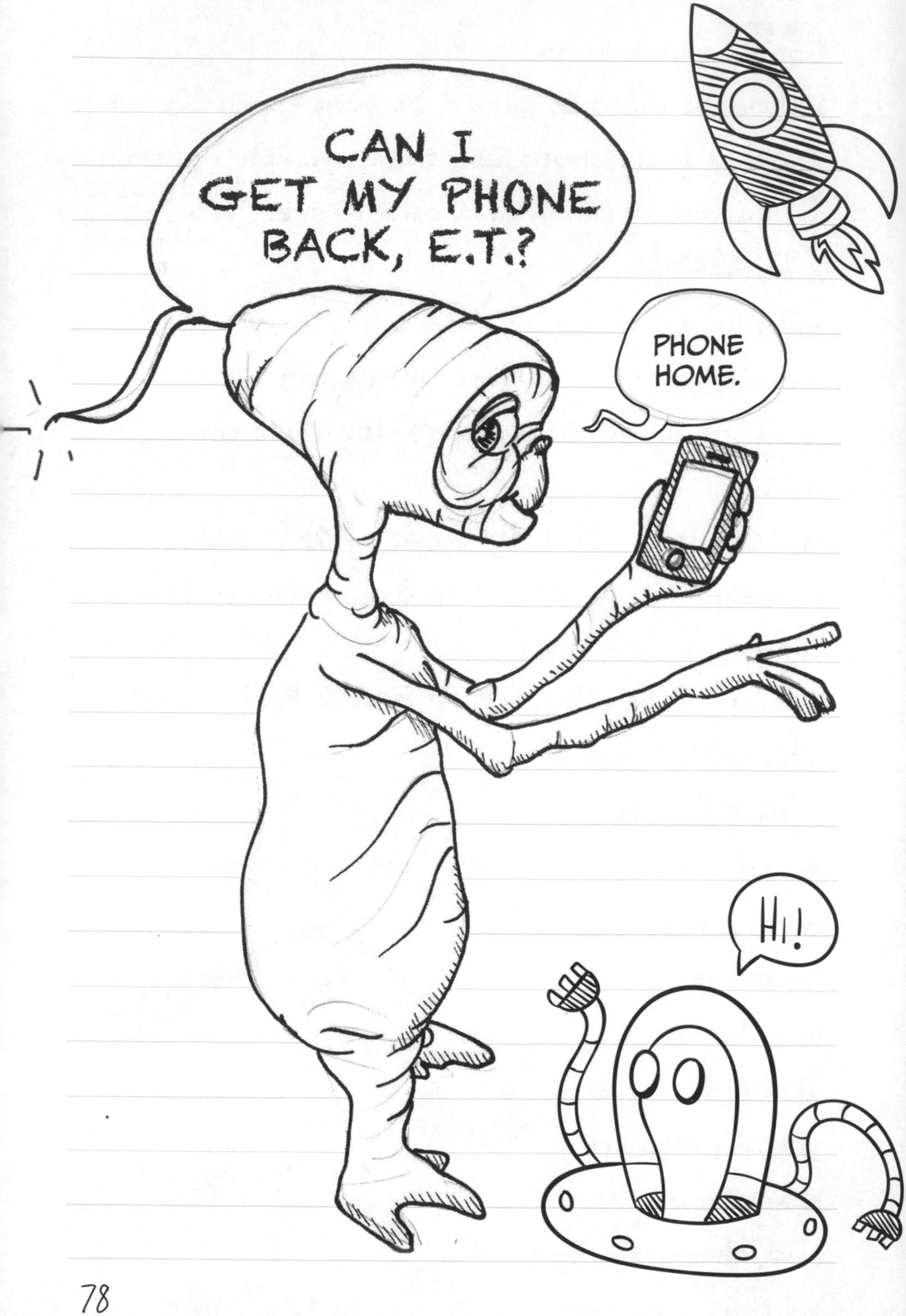
CAN I GET MY PHONE BACK, E.T.?
PHONE HOME.
HI!

But when I TRIED TO ASK for an explanation, he DISAPPEARED and I found myself all alone with my doubts.

October 21st

Teo's barking woke me up. MY LITTLE DOG was growling at an iPad. He would sometimes spend hours in front of the screen reading the newspaper online.

"At least they can't say that not even a dog will read the newspaper!" I told him, astonished to see him in the bedroom.

My father had packed him up and shipped him here via Fed Ex, and they had delivered him to us in less than 24 HOURS.

"But why didn't we bring him on the plane with us?" I asked. "There wasn't enough room for TEO and Alf," replied my father with his own peculiar logic. "AND i KNEW THAT TEO COULD GET HERE WITHOUT ME!"

I was happy to see my "certifiably unusual" dog again.

Before going down to the **HOTEL** restaurant for breakfast, I wanted to play with **TEO** a bit, but he looked much more interested in the online **SNOOPY** comics.

HE REALLY is PART OF THE FAMILY!

Like all of us, he lives in his own world!

TEO'S TRIP

I walked away from him, and a couple seconds later, I received a text on my iPhone. **Who could it be?**

I opened it and it was a text from **TEO** saying: "Good luck, Mr. Math!"

That was his way of encouraging and **SUPPORTING ME! How he manages to send texts without fingers is beyond me.**

The rest of the team and their parents were waiting for us downstairs.

I couldn't wait to see **BIG MIND KILL**. I loved looking into her eyes and talking to her. Just the thought of being close to her made my heart skip a beat. **SHE WAS LIKE A RAINBOW WITH EXTRA COLORS, SHE WAS MORE SPECIAL THAN SPECIAL!**

She was sitting at the table with her parents, who looked like they came right out of an art book. They were both artists and their clothing seemed to have all of the colors of a painter's palette.

I stared at **Big Mind Kill**, but her eyes were glued to a mathematics book she had brought with her. **SHE WAS STUDYING AS IF SHE HAD TO PASS THE MOST IMPORTANT EXAM OF HER LIFE.**

"This talent show is just a game!" I reminded her.

She raised her eyes and smiled at me.

"That's true, but I'm studying because I like to!" she said.

I was amazed by her determination and perseverance.

82

IT WAS LIKE SEEING MYSELF IN THE MIRROR, BUT IN A BEAUTIFUL BODY.

If my silence had been an emoji, she'd have seen a thousand hearts flying around her.

"Are you ready for our Hollywood Studios **TOUR**?" she asked me.

I was so happy she was interested in what I thought.

"Sure! We will get to see the sets of our favorite movies and tv shows!"

At that moment, I thought that I would even go to see the **TWILIGHT MOVIE** set with her, even though that movie scared me (at least what little of it I had seen).

After breakfast, I went to the restroom, because soon the **STUDIO TOUR** would begin. As I washed my hands at the sink, all of a sudden, right there in the mirror was **Darth Vader.**

I jumped back in shock!

"Heeeeeelp! You're back?"

I asked him after a moment of fear.

DARTH VADER was emotionless, as usual.

(His mask hides his feelings.)

"I've dropped by for a cameo!" he said.

I COULDN'T UNDERSTAND WHAT HE MEANT BY THAT.

"Just forget it, you brat. You're **LUCKY** I even thought of you, since I decided to stay away from **HOLLYWOOD**. I opened a pub in Ireland and I'm very **busy**."

"Ireland?" I asked, surprised.

"Just to avoid being involved in another bad movie. I'm afraid someone will put me in one of those **HORRIBLE SEQUELS**. Have you seen what happened to **Han Solo**?

NO ONE RESPECTS THE OLD MOVIE iCONS ANYMORE!"

How could I argue with that?

"YOU'RE RiGHT!

Maybe you should have a word with **George Lucas**," I suggested.

"You punk, forget about him! Remember, once a **NERD, ALWAYS A NERD**!"

"What do you mean?"

"Listen to the words of the Alien."

"How do you know about E.T.? Are you jealous?" I asked him.

"Even the **Power Rangers** have fans, you know. You can like him as much as you want, even if he looks like a **Teletubby** and couldn't even scare a newborn baby."

"Ok, I'll listen to what you have to say," I told him. **HE WAS MY FIRST MENTOR**, after all.

"Find your spaceship home and also the balance of the victory," he reminded me before vanishing.

That was exactly what E.T. had told me. **What did it mean?**

October 21st was absolutely one of the most beautiful days of my life, especially because all the people **I LOVE WERE THERE WITH ME** (from my parents to my friends).

THE CALIFORNIA SUN IS DIFFERENT FROM THE NEW YORK SUN. Where I live, you **CAN FEEL** an energy that can brighten the darkest streets, but in **LOS ANGELES** the sun brings colors and joy!

It was a typical day in **LA**, where the sun is the king who shines and makes all the inhabitants of the "kingdom" happy.

The TV network was giving us a tour of the studios.

However, we were a **TEAM OF KIDS** and we came from the other side of the country, so it wasn't going to be a typical **UNIVERAL STUDIOS TOUR**. They wanted to show us the **REAL**

HOLLYWOOD, SOMETHING THAT WOULD BE EVERY NERD'S DREAM!

Two really weird guides came to pick us up. One of them was a kind of stocky guy with an unkempt beard and the look of a wild man. He wore a black t-shirt and his baseball cap was backwards. He introduced himself: "**My name's Kevin**, and despite my good looks, I'm not **Justin Bieber**!"

My dad's eyes widened as soon as he saw him. The other guy was blond and he wore an unbuttoned jacket with a **BOB MARLEY** t-shirt underneath. He also wore a wool hat that definitely wasn't appropriate for the weather. "**My name's Jason**. Let's go. We'd better hurry, my fans are waiting!" he said somewhat arrogantly.

MY DAD FELL TO THE FLOOR IN AMAZEMENT.

I hurried over to make sure he was ok and after a moment he said: "Did you see who they are?"

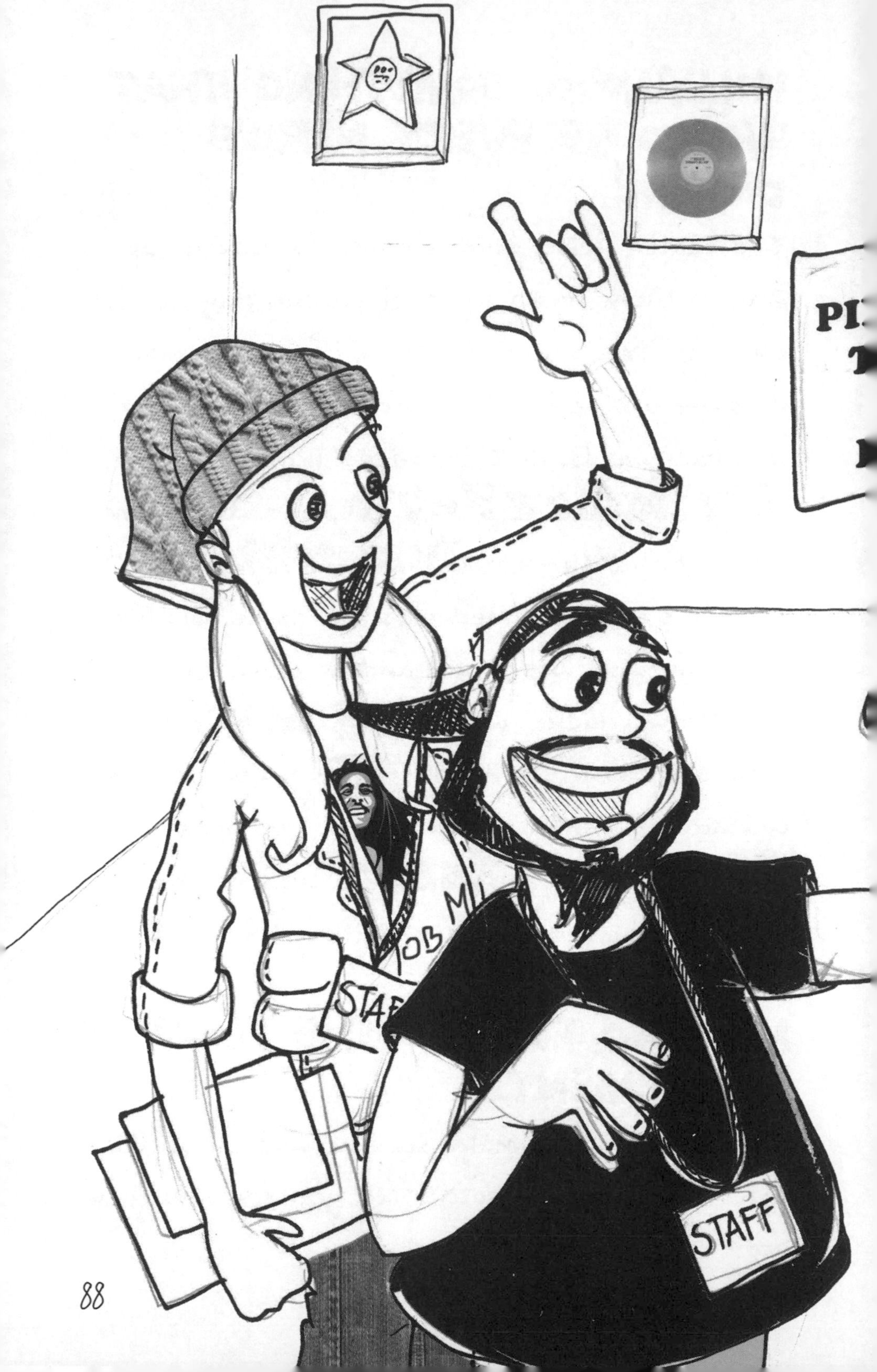
STAFF

I looked at them again, but saw nothing special, just two **HOLLYWOOD** dudes.

"They're actually **Jay and Silent Bob!**" said Dad.

"Who?" I asked, perplexed.

"**THEY'RE TWO SUPER COOL NERDS**, without them '**NEW NERDS**' wouldn't exist! They made history!"

"**Earth to Dad**," I shouted. "The '90s are over. Come back to us!" I was hoping that his craziness would stay locked in his brain for at least a few hours.

"**YOU DON'T UNDERSTAND!**

They were true icons! Nerds! A mirror image of all of us idiots in the '90s!"

OK, THIS WAS BEYOND ME, THERE'S NOTHING I COULD DO!

At that moment, Jason came over to him and said: "Come on, old man, get a move on and come with us... And if you're thinking that we're **JAY** and **SILENT BOB**, let me give you a news flash:

It's NERD TIME!

JAY & SILENT BOB
Who are they?

Dad mistook Kevin for Silent Bob, and Jason for Jay. Want to know who those two weirdos are? Dad loved them, and they were his idols. It's a nerd's duty to learn about them, even if their stories are not for kids.

Jay & Silent Bob are a couple of characters created by American moviemaker Kevin Smith. Smith, himself, plays Silent Bob, while Jason Mewes plays Jay. They became popular thanks to the movie Clerks (1994). Then they appeared in every single "View Askewniverse" movie, as well as Wes Craven's Scream 3 and the TV series Degrassi: The Next Generation.

Jay & Silent Bob are two guys from New Jersey who spend all their time hanging around outside a convenience store.

Jay's about 30 years old, and almost 6 feet tall. He has long, straight, blond hair, usually wears a wool hat, and dresses like a rapper.

Bob has a beard, and always wears a backwards baseball cap and a dark-green, wool coat, and hardly ever speaks. He's also a chain-smoker. The friends first met in front of the Quick Stop Groceries when they were kids. Despite being secondary characters in most of the films, they represent the connection between all the stories about their neighborhood and the people who live there. Since their scenes were so ridiculously funny, their creator gave them their own movie in 2001: Jay and Silent Bob Strike Back. In that movie, many of the characters from Kevin Smith's previous movies appear as secondary characters.

We are not them!" Then Kevin said, "THOSE TWO GUYS ARE EXTRAORDINARILY AWESOME AND INCREDIBLY CLEVER, THEY ARE NOT JUST TOUR GUIDES LIKE US. Right now, they are probably acting on the set of a huge movie production, as they deserve to be."

BUT, MY FATHER DIDN'T BELIEVE THEM.

He thought that they were both lying, but he humored them just because he loved the idea of spending some time with his **teenage idols.** So he got up off the ground and followed them.

"VERY WELL, we'll begin our tour at an old, legendary set, where you'll have the chance to admire ONE OF THE MOST BEAUTIFUL INVENTIONS IN MOTION PICTURE HISTORY," Kevin said.

He had awakened our curiosity, and when we opened the door to the sound stage, we found ourselves staring at the Delorean from BACK TO THE FUTURE.

"If you miserable, little monsters don't know what **Back to The Future** is, **HOLLYWOOD** is no place for you! This is not just a car, it's what allows **DOC BROWN** and **MARTY MCFLY** to travel through time!"

Still wearing the paper bag on his head, **NICHOLAS** went right up to the car and began petting it **AS IF IT WAS A LITTLE DOG.** **KEVIN** went up to him and tried to snatch the sack off of his head, but **GEORGE** immediately lowered his shoulders to block **KEVIN.**

George yelled.

"I want to see the alien hiding underneath that bag!" replied **KEVIN**, as though possessed.

"**ALIEN?** Has somebody seen an alien?" asked **DAD**, who had been totally absorbed in looking at the **DELOREAN** and had no idea what was going on.

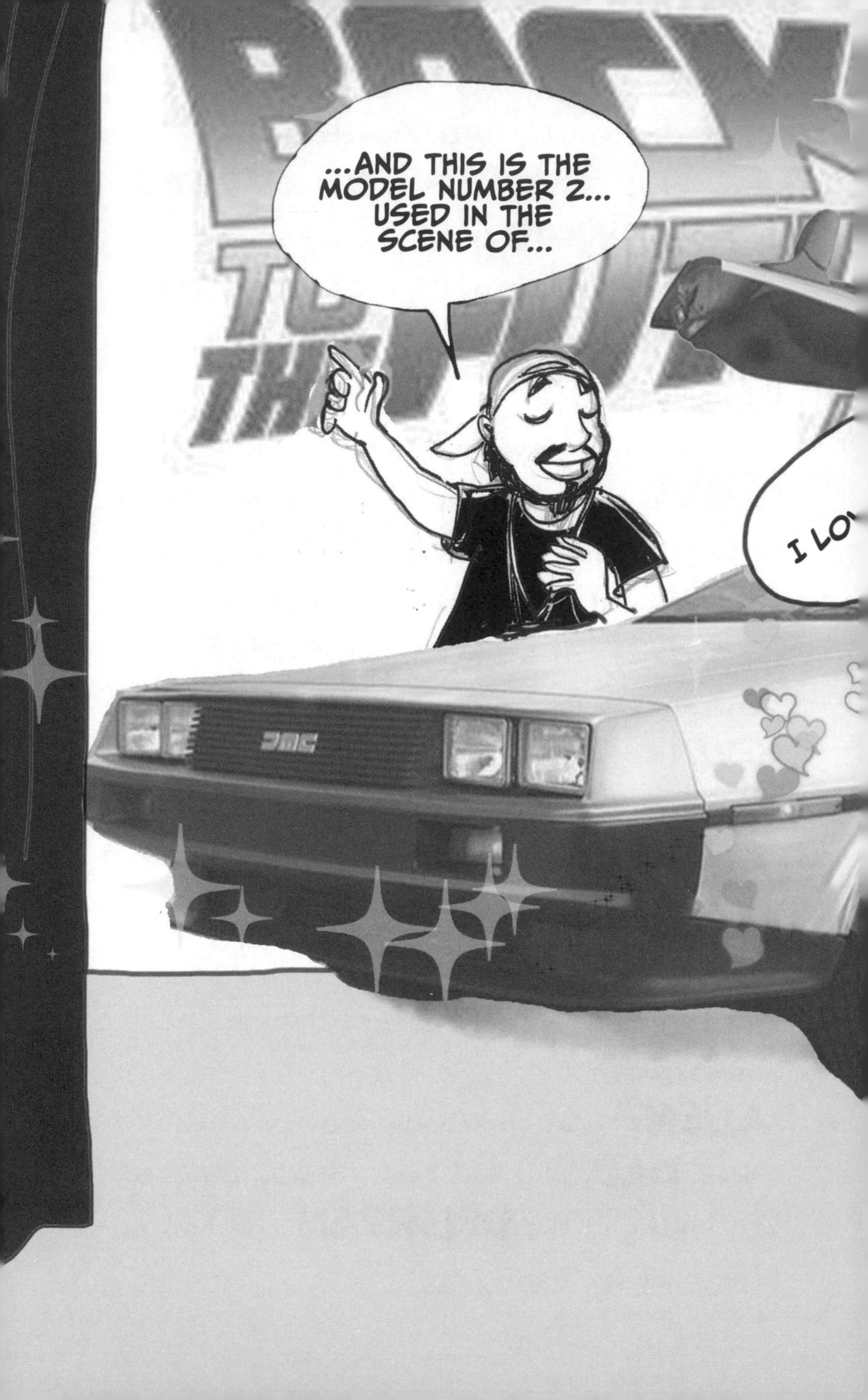
...AND THIS IS THE MODEL NUMBER 2... USED IN THE SCENE OF...

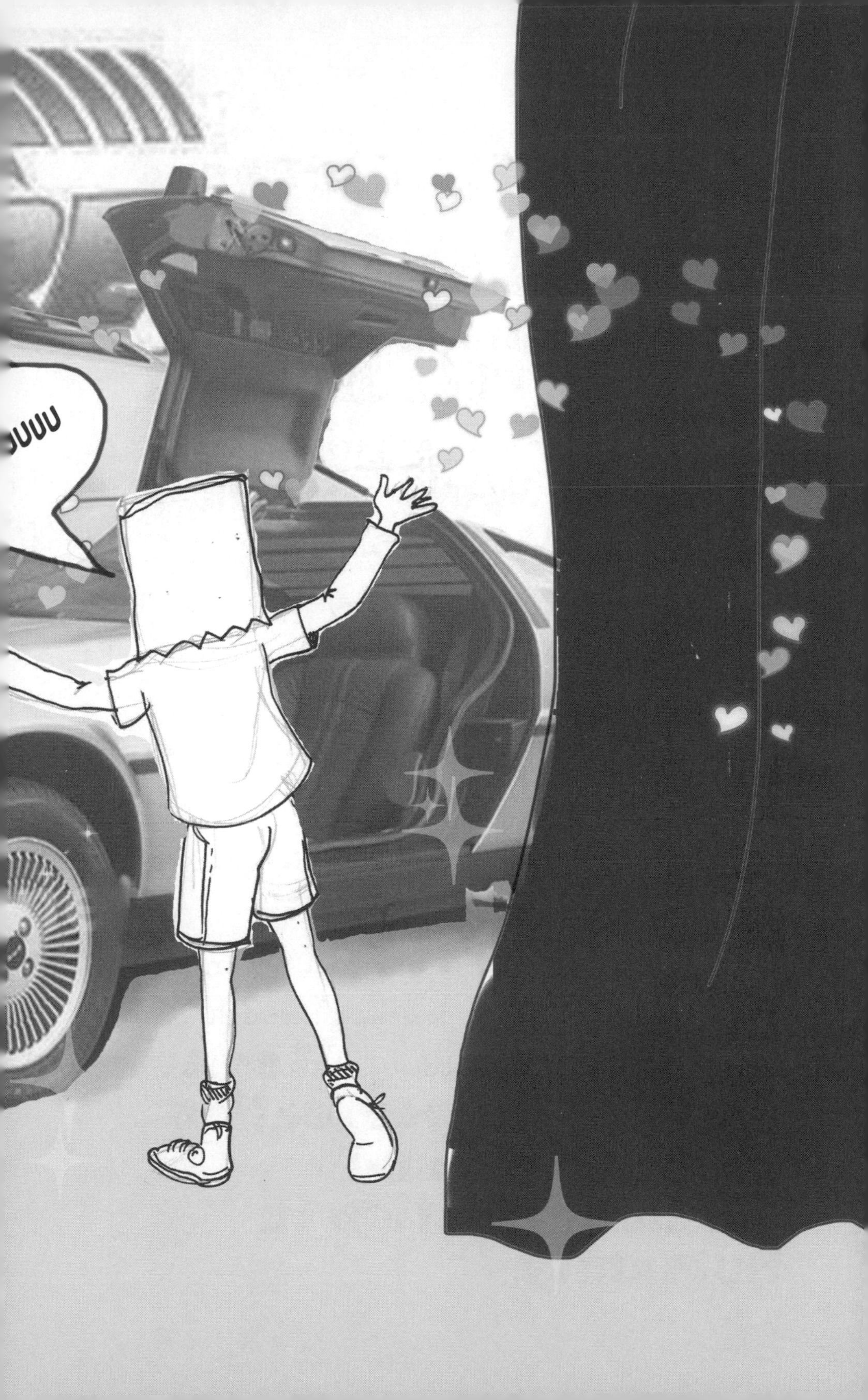
UUUU

"LET ME GO, I don't want you to see how I feel!" **NICHOLAS** yelled, and **KEVIN** let him go.

Ellen looked over at me.

NONE OF US HAD EVER ASKED WHY NICHOLAS DECIDED TO LIVE WITH A PAPER BAG OVER HIS HEAD, but now it was perfectly clear:

HE DIDN'T WANT ANYONE TO SEE HIS EMOTIONS.

He was probably hypersensitive, and kids like us sometimes can't understand emotions, so he didn't want to feel judged.

I'm not **SURE** if I was right or not, but I figured that Nicholas felt more comfortable and protected under that bag. He was my friend and I respected his choices.

"This **DELOREAN** is not just a car, it can take you on a journey through time," **KEVIN** said slowly. **"It can show us the perfection in the world and the imperfection in humanity."**

After we had spent 20 minutes in the world of **BACK TO THE FUTURE**, our two guides took us to another set where the real **Gizmo** was waiting for us. It was from **JOE DANTE'S** film, **Gremlins**.

"Before taking you to the sets of today's movies, we should first appreciate one of the past masterpieces of film," said **KEVIN**. **"Gizmo is a perfect creature**, a cross between a pet, an alien, and a human. **HE REPRESENTS INNOCENCE THAT MAKES ITSELF STRONG.**

Maybe some of you have never seen the movie, but **Gizmo** was a peculiar creature with certain rules that had to be followed. For instance, he must not be exposed to light, especially sunlight because that could kill him. Another rule is that **Gizmo** should never get wet, because water starts his reproductive cycle and so he would start to multiply. And, finally, he shouldn't be fed after midnight."

You don't Know what Mogwais are?

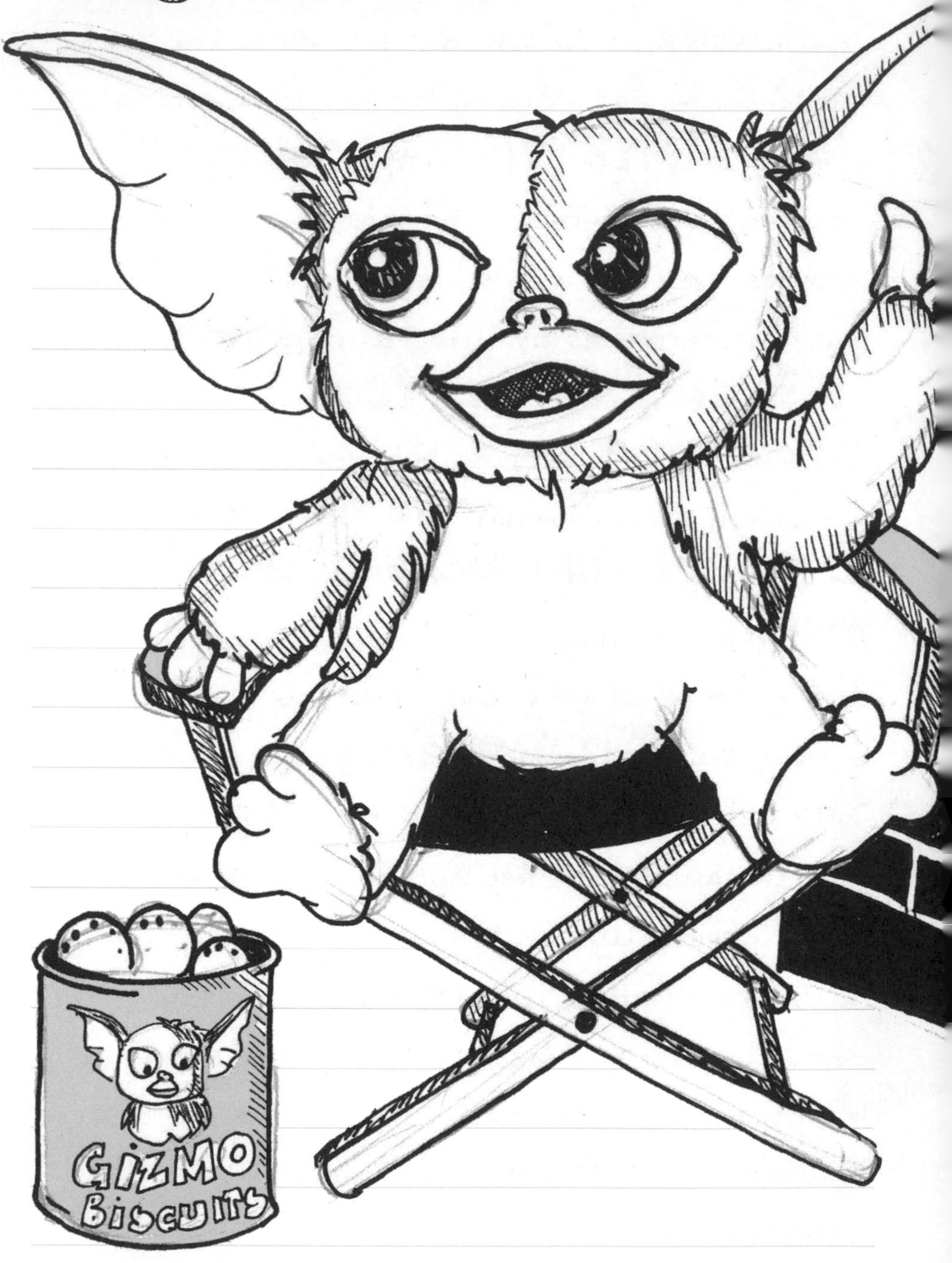
GIZMO
BISCUITS

NERD TIME!

HEY GUYS!

In 1943, Roald Dahl wrote a children's book titled "The Gremlins." Working with Disney Studios, he developed a screenplay, but it was never made into a movie. Chris Columbus was inspired by the idea and wrote a script that was more horror-driven. In it, Billy's mom gets killed by the Gremlins and her head is seen rolling down the stairs. In another scene, the family dog is eaten by the Gremlins, and in another, the Gremlins assault a McDonald's and eat all the customers instead of hamburgers. Finally, Gremlins was made into a less horrific and funnier movie in 1984 that was directed by Joe Dante, written by Chris Columbus, and produced by Steven Spielberg. The movie was hugely successful and praised by critics for its perfect blend of horror and comedy.

KEVIN opened the door to the set where the strange creature was kept. We were all astonished. **GEORGE'S** parents are both engineers who are fixated on symmetry and aren't very fond of **FANTASY MOVIES**. But, they were immediately captivated by **GIZMO'S** sweet nature. They'd never seen **JOE DANTE'S** movie, but their hearts melted when they saw the little Mogwai.

"That white spot on his right side: that's asymmetrical!" **GEORGE'S** Mom said. **SHE WAS RIGHT, OBVIOUSLY**, but I've never thought the world should be completely put into a **SYMMETRICAL ORDER**.

"But I like him anyway!" she added. **George** smiled because his parents had discovered how magical things that were "different" could be.

i WAS LOOKING FORWARD TO SEEING THE OTHER MOVIE SETS, and when we wondered what "world" they would take us to next, JASON signaled for us to be quiet.

We could hardly contain ourselves! Even Big Mind Kill was totally excited, despite usually being the one most in control of her emotions.

We followed JASON and KEVIN, and we SUDDENLY FOUND OURSELVES IN HOGWARTS, the school of wizardry and magic where most of the HARRY POTTER stories are set.

That's when we realized that we were having the most AMAZING AFTERNOON of our lives! We saw 4 PRIVET DRIVE, the DURSLEY'S HOUSE, and after that we saw the BURROW which was where the WEASLEY'S lived, which was a warm, cozy place.

They also took us to a corner of the studio that was part of the FORBIDDEN FOREST.

It was a thick forest that stretched out
from **HOGWARTS** for miles, and at the end

THE SET OF HARRY POTTER WAS A WINDOW INTO FANTASY BROUGHT TO LIFE.

of it was Hagrid's Hut. In the forest, there were lots of magical creatures, including

THESTRALS, UNICORNS, CENTAURS, ACROMANTULAS (led by ARAGOG, the talking spider that HAGRID would hide in HOGWARTS when he was still a student there) and many other characters. We then moved to the sets of **Divergent**, **STAR WARS**, STAR TREK, **The Hunger Games**, and we even saw the set where they were about to shoot a music video for **ARIANA GRANDE.** HOLLYWOOD REALLY WAS THE HOME OF DREAMS AND STARS!

Our minds were full of fantastic images. I asked Kevin if he could show us E.T. But he told me that the creature conceived of by **STEVEN SPIELBERG** and created by **CARLO RAMBALDI** was locked safely away in a studio that no one had access to. I was disappointed, because it would've been amazing to touch the real E.T., instead of the one I had seen in my dreams last night. Was what I saw real or just something my brain had invented?

104

I was tired, but before going back to the hotel, I wanted to talk to **BIG MIND KILL**. No one was around and I wanted to spend a little time with her.

"Awesome, right?" I asked her, talking about what we had seen.

"Awesome!" she answered with no hesitation. And then she added:

"**Like you!**"

When I watch tutorials on Youtube, I usually put them on repeat. Well, that's what I wanted to do with our conversation... watch it infinite times, just to make sure I understood her words correctly.

BIG MIND KILL just paid me a compliment and I turned as gooey as a

roasted marshmallow.

October 22nd

The day had come. It was the showdown. Breakfast at the hotel had been ready for quite some time... but we were not. **EVEN IF OUR MINDS WERE FOCUSED ON THE COMPETITION**, we were in a trance. We were tense and silent. In a few hours, we'd challenge the **EVIL AVENGERS** and the talent show would make us famous all over the world.

OUR PARENTS TRIED TO CHEER US UP because they would soon be sitting in the audience. **The producers asked us to choose our costumes for the competition.** We had no idea what our rivals would wear, but **ELLEN** had already picked up some **ANGRY BIRDS** costumes.

We looked ridiculous.

GEORGE wore the costume of **CHUCK**, the triangular yellow bird that will zoom straight like a bullet if you touch him in flight. He asked ELLEN: "**COULDN'T YOU FIND ANYTHING AT LEAST A LITTLE BIT SCARY? SOMETHING TO FRIGHTEN THE OTHER TEAM A LITTLE? THAT COULD WORK!**"

Maybe he was right.

We didn't look strong or determined. In these costumes, we wouldn't scare a bug.

"**IT'S A STRATEGY!**" my sister insisted.

She was wearing Red's costume, the group leader. "If you look at me, **I look powerless**, just like Red. But remember, he was the one who understood what the pigs were up to!" she said.

WE LOOKED FOOLISH and, even worse, our ideas seemed incomprehensible, even to ourselves.

Big Mind Kill, who didn't like **Angry Birds**, was given the all-black costume of Bomb. So she said: "**THIS COSTUME DOESN'T MAKE ANY SENSE...**"

GEORGE

BIG M

NICHOLAS

RUBIK

The Terrible P

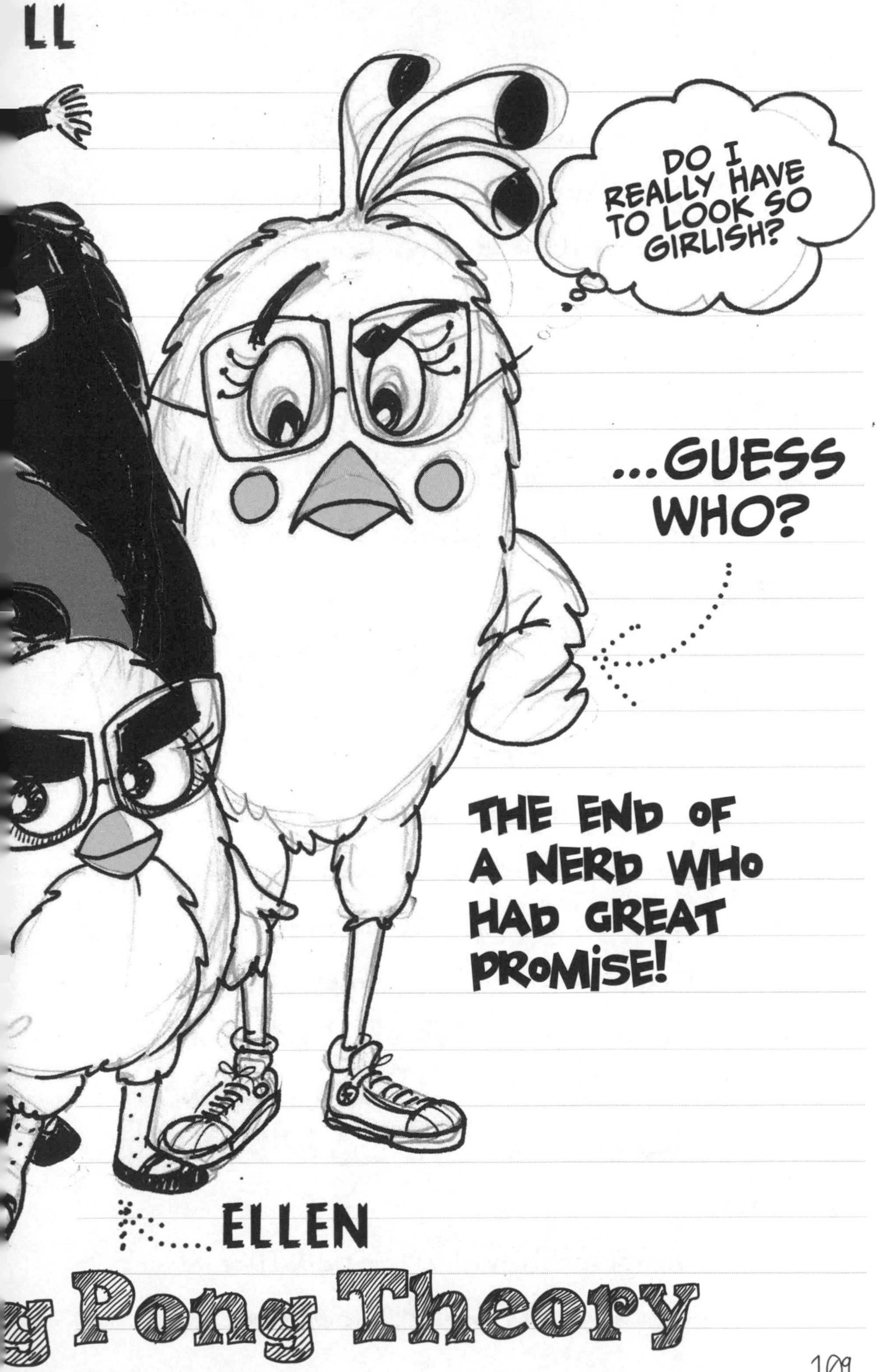
LL
DO I REALLY HAVE TO LOOK SO GIRLISH?
...GUESS WHO?
THE END OF A NERD WHO HAD GREAT PROMISE!
ELLEN
g Pong Theory

ELLEN had already anticipated this and she immediately replied: "**Exactly like Bomb**, who explodes upon landing, you will be useful in destroying the 'hard objects!'"

NOOOO!

My sister was speaking **LIKE A CARTOON**:

Heeeelp!

Nicholas wore the costume of Bubbles: a small, orange bird that swells up like a giant balloon when touched, and then deflates quickly leaving feathers all around. My shy friend decided not to complain, but **ELLEN** said to him: "I KNOW WHAT YOU'RE THINKING... AND YOU, JUST LIKE BUBBLES, WILL LET GO OF YOUR SHYNESS AND BECOME A GIANT!"

I had the worst costume. I looked like a chicken wearing **MATILDA'S** costume.

When touched while flying, **that bird has the power to shoot eggs like bombs**.

Our parents stared at us as if **BIGFOOT** was standing in front of them.

Only my dad didn't react, because he was literally captivated by reading the newspaper online. In perfect 1980s **COMIC BOOK** style, he suddenly exclaimed:

"GOLLY!"
We all burst out laughing.

"This isn't funny!" he said with a worried look on his face. **"LAST NIGHT THE STUDIOS WERE ROBBED!**

A lot of movie props that are loved by **NERDS** all over the world have been stolen, including the **DELOREAN** and **DARTH VADER'S** helmet. Not only that, but the burglars also broke into **GEORGE LUCAS'** house and stole R2D2 and C3PO."

We stopped laughing. These things were all treasures to nerds. While the **DELOREAN** couldn't actually travel through time, it was way more valuable to the nerds who loved these movies. **THIS WAS A TRAGEDY INFLICTED ON THE WORLD OF FILM AND TELEVISION.**

"They also stole **HARRY POTTER'S** magic wand — the original one!" **DAD** continued, in shock. He'd been a **nerd** and he understood the value of **THOSE PROPS**, which was not something you could measure in dollars and cents. They were mythical! **BIG MIND KILL** came over and hugged me and said something I'd later remember:

YOU'VE SAVED AN ENTIRE GALAXY AND NOW... NOW YOU DO NOTHING?!

PRISONER TRANSPORTATION

AT50

"**WHO WOULD STEAL THINGS THAT ONLY NERDS LOVE?**"

A few hours later, we entered the Studio.

I was sad because years of dreams had been stolen and they might never be seen again. **Simon**, the show's creator, got up on stage and reminded us that more than **7 million** people watched **AMERICA LOVES TALENT.**

I came back to the present and decided to forget about the sad news. I was thirsty and asked where I could find something to drink. **KEVIN** and **JASON** were on the set and they pointed out the way. "**DOWN THE HALL, TO THE RIGHT, YOU'LL FIND A VENDING MACHINE**," they said in unison. I dragged myself down there, hoping a soda would cheer me up. Right next to the machine, there was **E.T.**

"Here you are again!" he said with an arrogance that I never thought an **alien** could have. "**HAVE YOU SEARCHED FOR THE SPACESHIP HOME AND THE BALANCE OF VICTORY?**"

"You, again?"

"Time flies, and if you want to, too, look for the spaceship and the **BALANCE OF VICTORY!**"

I couldn't understand what he meant. I just wanted to win!

"**DARTH VADER** was far more talkative and didn't make fun of me with these stupid riddles," I replied.

"The sky's ready, but we need the **BALANCE OF VICTORY!**" E.T. continued.

I thought the alien had a serious problem communicating.

"**PHIL!** Phil the Nerd, where is he?" Jason yelled. **The director was looking for me** and I didn't realize how late it was. I took my soda and ran to my seat, ready to start fighting against the **EVIL AVENGERS**.

"We're about to go live. Kids, do you know what that means? **IT'S LIKE LIVE STREAMING**, so if you make a mistake, we do not repeat. Here, everything is one take!" **QUENTIN**, the director, yelled.

He never forgot the **Oscar** he'd won 10 years ago.

116

The lights went off... ▪ ▪ ▪ and a voice invited

us to remain silent. The show's theme music

started and the lights came on to reveal

RIHANNA. She was the hostess of **AMERICA**

LOVES TALENT. She looked beautiful

and she loved repeating to each contestant:

"Smile, smile, YOU'RE ON

AMERICA LOVES TALENT!"

She was a bit over the top,

but very nice, and even tonight she said

her typical phrase: "You people at

home, smile, you people

in the audience, smile,

HOLLYWOOD

"THIS IS HOLLYWOOD, LAND OF DREAMS. SOME DREAMS COME TRUE, AND SOME DON'T, BUT KEEP ON DREAMING!"
FROM THE FILM PRETTY WOMAN, BY GARRY MARSHALL.

Do you Know the true story of E.T.? NERD TIME!

One night, a mysterious spaceship lands in the middle of
a California forest and out come some alien botanists who
start collecting samples of the vegetation. Government
agents suddenly appear and the aliens flee back into their
spaceship and they take off, leaving one alien behind,
unnoticed.

Meanwhile, in the suburbs of Los Angeles, a nine-year-old
boy named Elliott, spends the evening with his older brother
Michael and his friends playing Dungeons & Dragons. When
he goes out for pizza, Elliott hears some noises in a closet.
At first he thinks that it is his own dog, but it turns out to
be the alien, who runs away. Even though his
family doesn't believe him, Elliott leaves
candy scattered in the forest in order
to attract the alien. One night the
extraterrestrial goes to Elliott with
all the candies, and the boy hides the
alien in his room to keep it secret from
his family.

and all you competitors, smile... everyone

SMILE!

Because you're on **AMERICA LOVES TALENT**!"

There was a big applause, then she continued.

"Today's match is going to be incredible... a

bunch of harmless kids versus a scary team of

adults! WHO WILL BE THE MOST TALENTED IN

MATHEMATICS? **SMILE**, because it's time to

meet the teams!" **RIHANNA** said.

"Here are the **Ping Pong Theory**

from **NEW YORK CITY**, led by sweet, little

Ellen!" the host announced.

MY SISTER LOOKED LIKE SHE WANTED TO THROW A CAKE IN HER FACE, because she hated being

called sweet and little. Her angry look

showed how disapproving she was of being

described that way.

"SMILE,

smile sweetie, let's have a round of applause for **ELLEN, GEORGE, NICHOLAS, BIG MIND KILL** and **Phil the Nerd!**" the host continued. **ELLEN** swallowed her anger and played along. The warm reception caught us by surprise.

Our costumes and young ages made us sympathetic to the studio audience... and probably to the people at home, as well. **ELLEN'S** strategy wasn't as crazy as we thought!

"**ARE YOU READY?** It's time to meet the **Evil Avengers!** They're a team of adults, led by **MR. GRAY'S** genius. They are nightmares from movies and TV. **SKELETOR, MISS SCREAM, MORTIMER AKA THE WALKING DEAD**, Venom Slim, and **MR. GRAY** are here to humiliate

the poor, hapless **Ping Pong Theory!**"

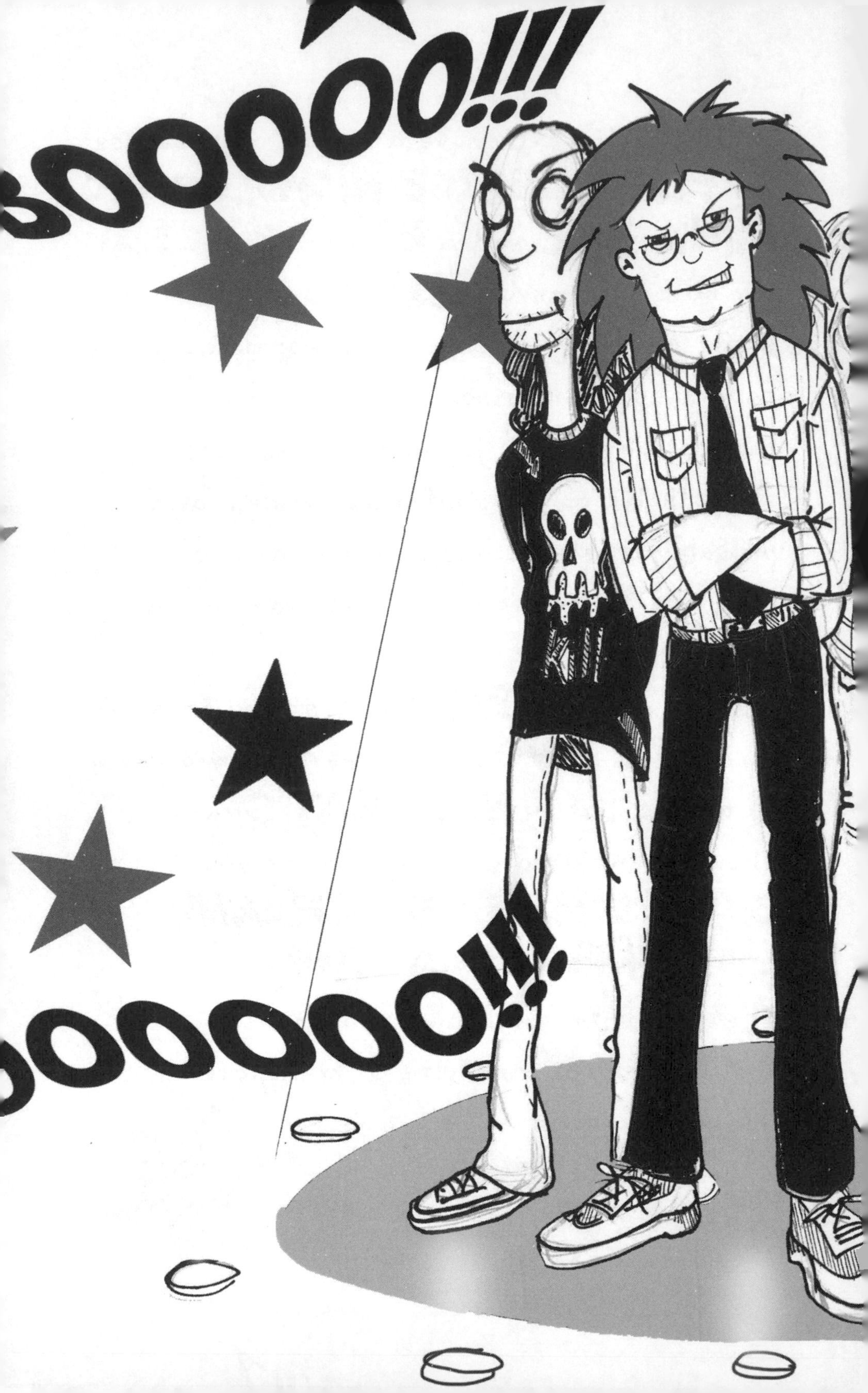
OOOOOO!!!
OOOOOOO!!!

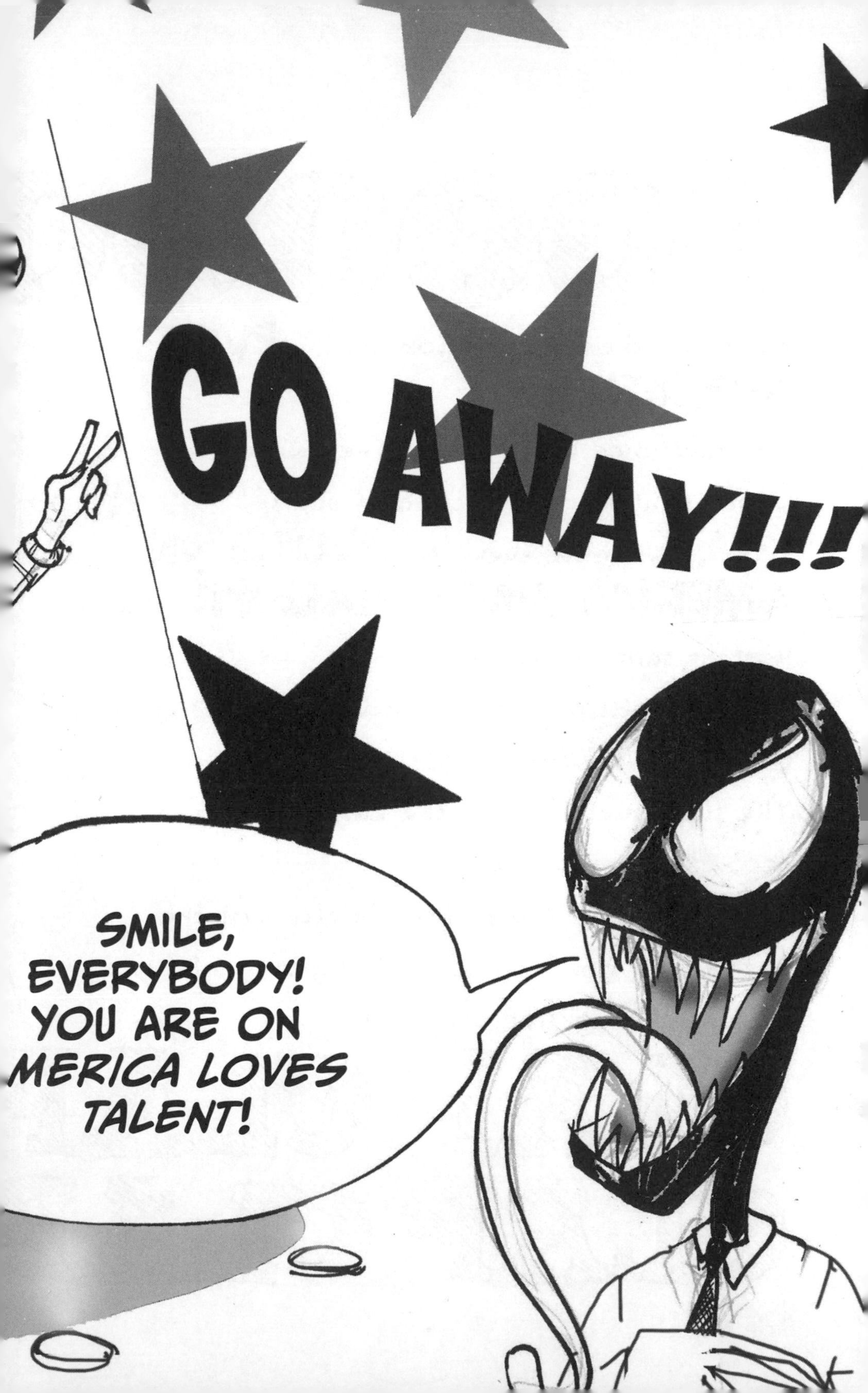
GO AWAY!!!
SMILE, EVERYBODY! YOU ARE ON MERICA LOVES TALENT!

A loud

followed the introduction of the **EVIL AVENGERS.**

The audience hated them. They were

unpleasant know-it-alls and scary.

"**SMILE**, smile everyone! **YOU'RE ON AMERICA LOVES TALENT!**" our

hostess said again.

The competition started and the judges took

their seats behind the desk.

The first question was the easiest. We had 15

seconds to answer it.

Rihanna read: "Given the equation of the

parabola $y = x^2 + x$, find the tangent lines

passing through the origin O."

NICHOLAS smiled and wrote the answer
in less than 2 seconds.

The judges considered it to be correct and gave us the first score.

The audience began cheering enthusiastically: **"PING PONG THEORY!"**

That was a really good start and it was all because of our intensive training and preparation!

The second question that **RIHANNA** asked caught us by surprise, so we stopped our celebrating and went silent.

"At what point does the parabola of the equation $y = (x - 2)^2$ become tangent to the x-axis?" she asked.

It was one of the questions you'd find on a University admission test for **Engineering** and, even if we had figured it out, we would have never answered as fast as the **EVIL AVENGERS** did.

As soon as they were given the points, **VENOM SLIM** burst out in a terrifying laugh that caused my sister to shiver. **THOSE GUYS WERE REALLY SCARY AND WELL-TRAINED.**

There was a chance that our talent might not be enough to defeat them. **But with concentration and determination, maybe we could do it.**

Any distraction would come at a terrible price.

RIHANNA got nearer to the camera, her gorgeous face in a close-up, and announced the **COOL CLIP MOMENT.** Every team was supposed to show a video for the judges to consider in giving bonus points for creativity.

"THE AUDIENCE WOULD LIKE TO GET TO KNOW YOU BETTER! You're all tied up for now, but one team can take the lead. It's **time** for you to show us something funny and creative. **Smile,** competitors and audience: it's time for some **COOL VIDEOS!** Let's start with the **Ping Pong Theory**," **RIHANNA** said breathlessly.

ELLEN stood up from her seat, took the remote control and played our clip.

In the video, we were in a **3D CARTOON** wearing superhero tights and fighting against some **Transformers**-like beings. At the end of the battle, **ELLEN** gave our enemies some ice cream cones and we danced together on a beautiful **Malibu** beach. **THE CLIP WAS SUNNY** and bright, and **SHOWED THE LOVE**

WE HAD FOR EACH OTHER,

and for our adversaries. In other words,

the competition was a game!

The audience appreciated our playful
and fun attitude.

ICE CREAM FOR EVERYBODY!

PEACE & LOVE

The judges stood up and showed us their scores: all 10s!

We had gotten the highest score possible, and the **EVIL AVENGERS** could only hope to match our own score and end in a tie for the second round.

MR. GRAY WASN'T LIKEABLE LIKE ELLEN WAS, AND DIDN'T EVEN TRY TO SMILE AT THE AUDIENCE.

He seemed angry. He didn't appreciate the fact that we were in **HOLLYWOOD,** HAVING FUN ON ONE THE MOST WATCHED SHOWS IN THE WORLD.

He took the remote control and started the video clip that the **EVIL AVENGERS** had prepared.

Their video took place at my school.

It started with a piece of text:

"PREPARE YOURSELVES TO MEET A TERRIBLE MONSTER!"

All of us in the **Ping Pong Theory**

started laughing, because the **EVIL AVENGERS** had prepared a Horror Clip that the jury was sure to hate.

WHAT FOLLOWED WERE SOME IMAGES FROM MY SCHOOL AND A TITLE CARD THAT SAID: "**Here hides the terrifying creature that, like a snake, hides from everything and everyone.**"

Then my face appeared.

WHAT WAS i DOiNG IN THAT ViDEO?

The scene showed me in the **i.T.** classroom hacking into the school computer and changing my grades from **GOOD** to **EXCELLENT**.

A final text in the video stated what they and the world thought of me now: "**PHIL THE NERD** is a fraud!

BOOOO

Phil THE NERD IS A LIAR!"

THE BOO'S FROM THE AUDIENCE FELT LIKE POISONED ARROWS.

The whole situation had turned upside down.
and **MR. GRAY** had managed to get the
audience to hate me.

SIMON, the chief juror, stood up and said:
"THE SHOW'S OVER FOR YOU. YOU AND YOUR
TEAM ARE OUT!

WE DON'T LIKE LIARS AND IMPOSTORS!"

What I saw on **GEORGE, NICHOLAS, BIG
MIND KILL**, and **ELLEN'S** faces was a
huge disappointment for having lost a great
opportunity, and even worse, for trusting the
wrong person.

OOOO!!!

How could I ever explain to them that **MR. GRAY** was the one **WHO HAD LED ME INTO DOING WHAT I DID?** **I WAS TIRED OF THE INJUSTICES AND HAD TRIED TO FIX THINGS.** But that had proven useless and my attempt at revenge had just made everything worse.

At that moment, **RIHANNA CALLED THE CAMERAS OVER TO HER** and said: "We have on the line the **PRINCIPAL** of **PHIL'S SCHOOL.**

He'd like to talk about our Nerd!" Here came old **PRINCIPAL DONALD**, another person who was quick to condemn. He was one of those people who only seemed to be **happy** when

132

SMILE, EVIL AVENGERS! SMILE! YOU'VE MANAGED TO GET THE *PING PONG THEORY* OUT OF THE COMPETITION.

he could judge someone else. "Phil, you've always been a model student, but I have no choice. **i AM SUSPENDING YOU FROM SCHOOL FOR A WEEK!** You've proven to be a huge disappointment, and obviously your final grades will be **AFFECTED BY YOUR BEHAVIOR!**"

The audience applauded, **AND NO ONE SEEMED TO BE INTERESTED IN TRYING TO UNDERSTAND WHY i'D DONE WHAT i DID.**

133

STRANGE BUT TRUE...

Did you know that in Italy, November 17th is Black Cat Day? It's a day dedicated to defending black cats from superstitions and prejudice. The celebration was created by the IADAE (Italian Association in Defense of Animals and the Environment).

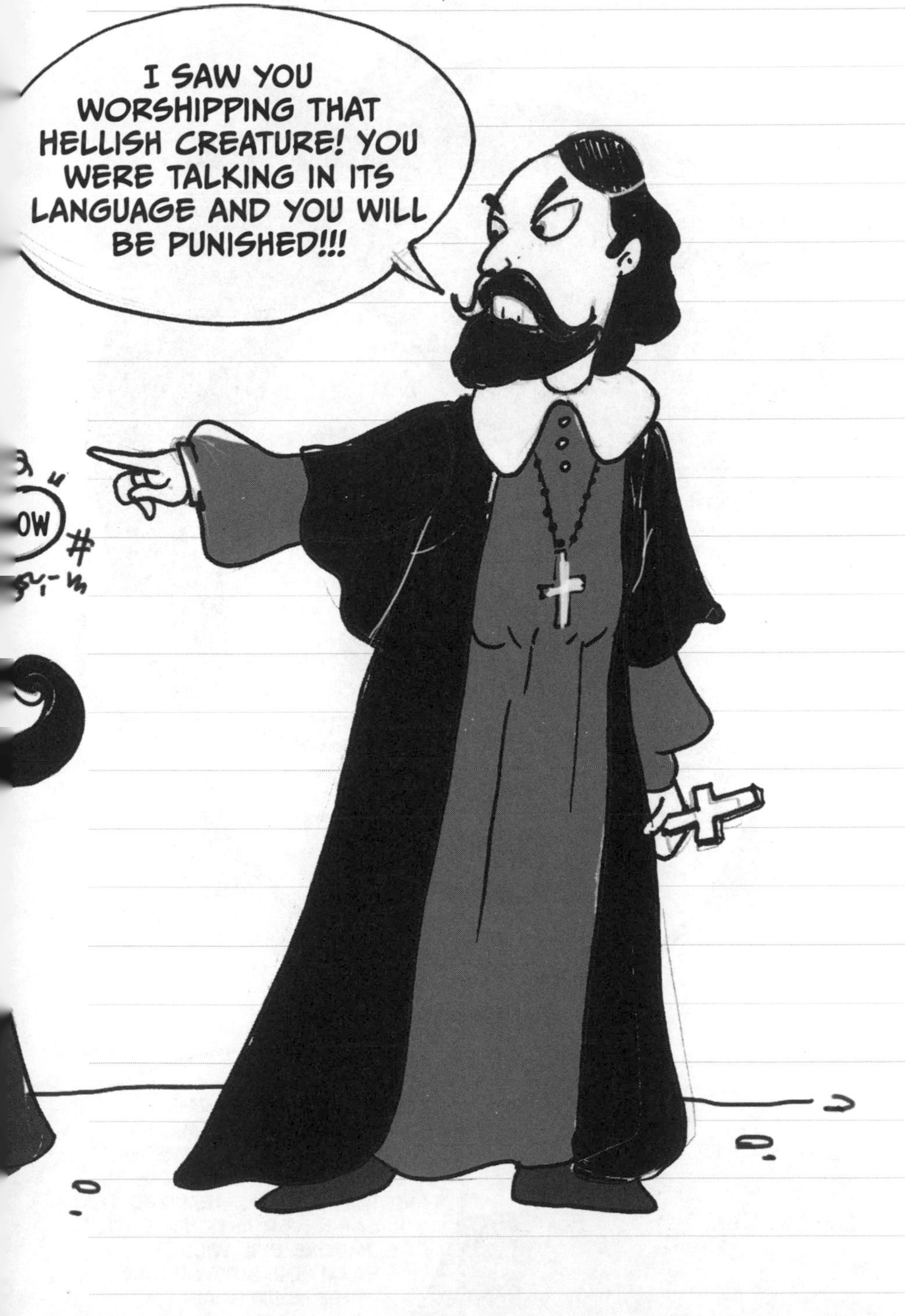
I SAW YOU WORSHIPPING THAT HELLISH CREATURE! YOU WERE TALKING IN ITS LANGUAGE AND YOU WILL BE PUNISHED!!!

Phil's Diary

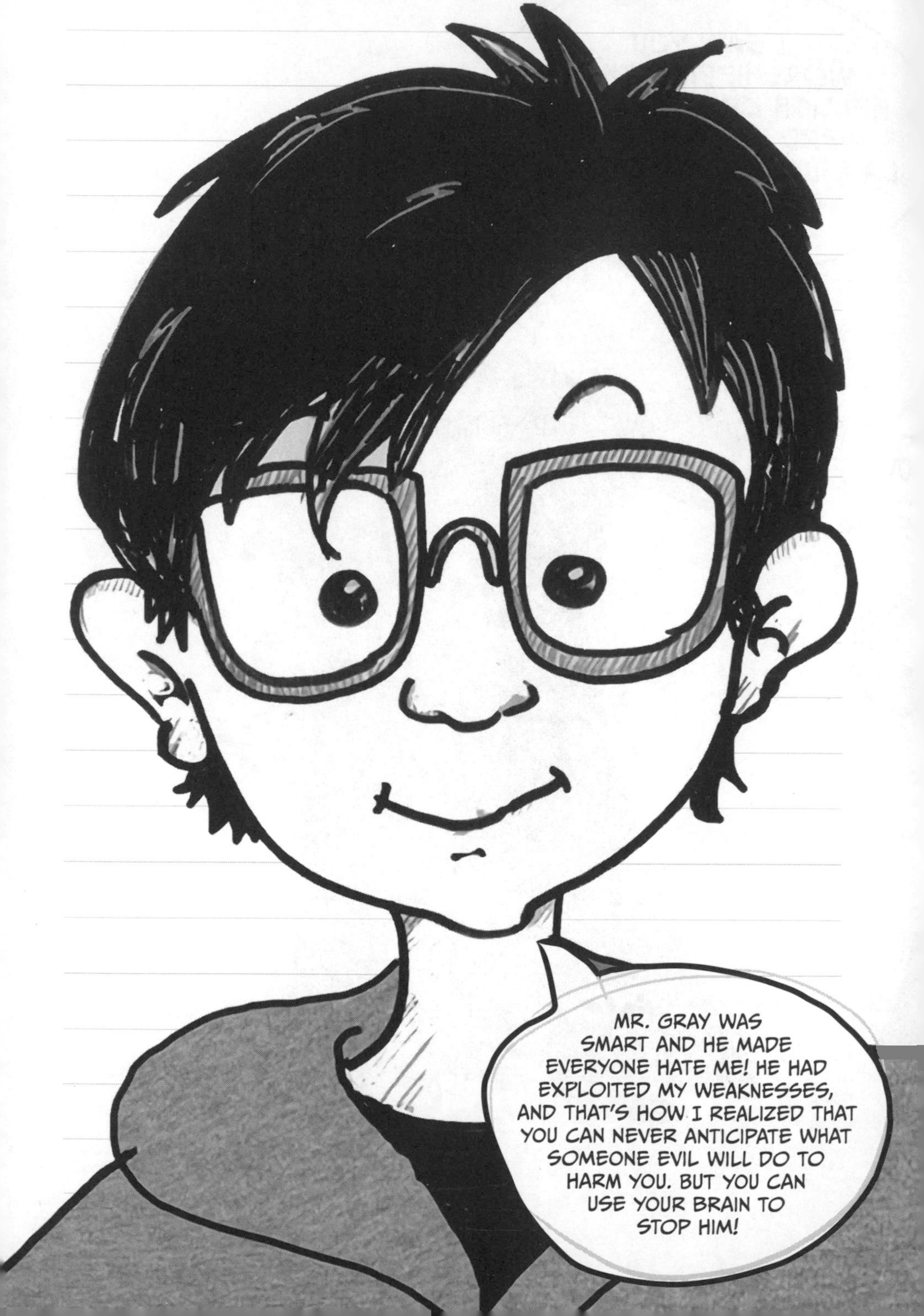
MR. GRAY WAS SMART AND HE MADE EVERYONE HATE ME! HE HAD EXPLOITED MY WEAKNESSES, AND THAT'S HOW I REALIZED THAT YOU CAN NEVER ANTICIPATE WHAT SOMEONE EVIL WILL DO TO HARM YOU. BUT YOU CAN USE YOUR BRAIN TO STOP HIM!

EPILOGUE

The Balance of Victory

ALBERT EINSTEIN SAID:
"IF YOU JUDGE A FISH BY ITS
ABILITY TO CLIMB A TREE,
IT WILL LIVE ITS WHOLE LIFE
BELIEVING THAT IT IS STUPID."
SO, DON'T JUDGE ME FOR MY
MISTAKES... BUT FOR WHAT I
WILL DO FROM NOW ON.

WE WERE IN OUR HOTEL, ABOUT TO HAVE DINNER BEFORE LEAVING THE FOLLOWING DAY.

My family and I were shunned by my friends and their families. They wouldn't look at or talk to us. Even **Big Mind Kill** didn't want me to get close to her.

"200 texts on WhatsApp and not a single reply!" I yelled to her.

SHE JUST IGNORED ME.

I was as sad as a scoop of ice cream without a cone, or an ocean without a fish.

My sister asked me to follow her and we left the hotel restaurant.

Outside at the swimming pool, she put some folders on a deckchair.

"What do you want?" I asked, a bit scared.

She gave me a print-out from the webpage **"YOUNG NERDS** of the '80s and '90s."

"Read!" She said. **"THIS WEBSITE LISTS ALL THE NAMES OF THE MOST FAMOUS NERDS** of the 1980s and the 1990s, when **MOM** and **DAD** were still normal people!"

I read the list of names, but they were all unknown to me, except **JASON** and **KEVIN**.

"Who are they and what's this got to do with me?" I asked, a little annoyed.

"You fool, look at that picture: the guy who is talking to **JASON** and **KEVIN**, the one with hair exactly like *Mr. Gray's* hair. But see, it says his name is '**RAYMOND MACCARTHY**.' This means either the website is wrong or **MR. GRAY** isn't who he says he is." **ELLEN** was proud of herself.

SHE WAS RIGHT!

GREAT!

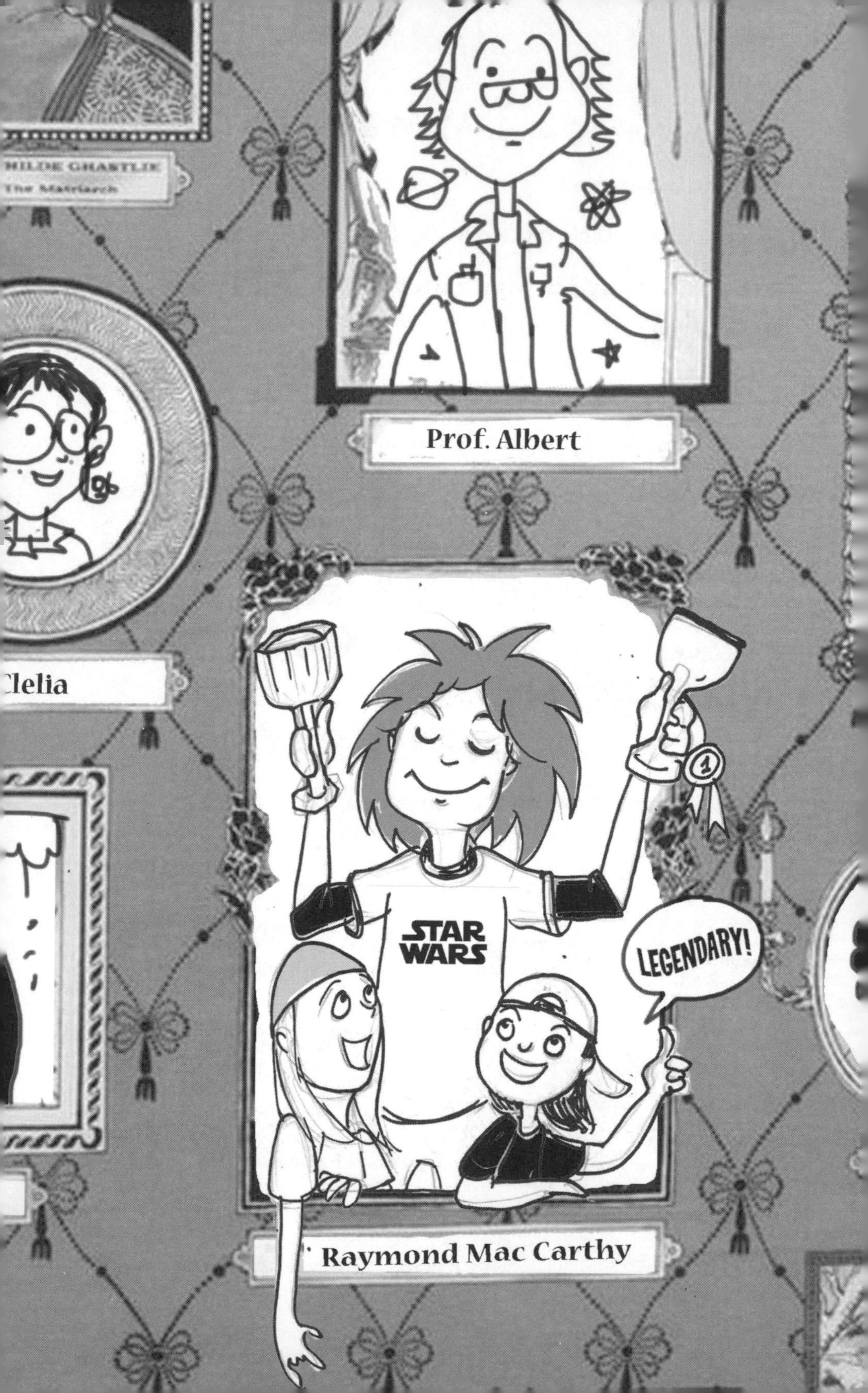
HILDE GHASTLIE
The Matriarch
Prof. Albert
Clelia
STAR WARS
LEGENDARY!
Raymond Mac Carthy

Prof. Tobery

Blacky sisters

If **MR. GRAY** was really **RAYMOND MACCARTHY**... that meant that he was the impostor!

But why was he pretending to be someone else?

Then I thought about what **BIG MIND KILL** had said: "Who would steal things only **nerds loved?**"

Darn!

WHO WAS THE NERD IN THE PHOTOGRAPH?

MR. GRAY! Or whatever his real name was.

"I've got it! Sister, you're a genius! **MR. GRAY Is ACTUALLY MACCARTHY,** and he was the nerd who broke into the studios and into Lucas' house and stole the props. Those are treasures to nerds and only a nerd would want to steal all of them. And it's clear that **Mr. Gray**, himself, was one! This photograph proves it. We have to find out where he hid the loot, who he really is, and how to go public with all of this before going back to New York."

"LET'S CALL THE REST OF THE TEAM AND JASON AND KEVIN. THEY KNEW RAYMOND MACCARTHY AND THEY CAN HELP US!" ELLEN concluded.

The rest of the team managed to sneak away from their parents after they got the call from **ELLEN**.

"It all comes down to our nerd pride!" stated **GEORGE**.

"I've already sent a WhatsApp text to **JASON** and they are on their way," **NICHOLAS** said out of the blue.

"How come you have Jason's cell phone number?" **BIG MIND KILL** asked.

"After he tried to take the paper bag off my head, I apologized and told him that if he wanted to see my face he could, but not in front of so many people. HE UNDERSTOOD AND SAID NO PROBLEM. He gave me his number in case I needed him. AND NOW WE DO NEED HIM!" NICHOLAS answered.

KEVIN AND JASON ARRIVED IN THEIR OLD, BEAT UP BUICK ROARING LIKE A VOLCANO ABOUT TO EXPLODE. Even our parents came out of the restaurant to hear what they had to tell us.

We showed them the article and KEVIN said: "That's Raymond MacCarthy. I haven't seen him in ages. HE USED TO BE A NERD AND HE WAS THE MOST UNPLEASANT GEEK EVER. He was a know-it-all and he thought he was superior to everyone in the whole world just because of the things he knew. HE WAS REALLY WELL EDUCATED, but then everybody stayed away from him, and that's when **HE STARTED TO HATE THE OTHER NERDS.** They kept him at a distance because he was **very competitive** and his snobby attitude made him unbearable. Everybody thought that 'Mr. Intelligence' was nothing but a joke. He was an icon at the beginning, but he ended up alone.

iT WAS iNEVITABLE!
HE WASN'T SOCIABLE, SO NO ONE WANTED TO SPEND TIME WITH HIM!"

We were all surprised.

"Are you sure about his name?" I asked.

"**MACCARTHY**, I remember it well. **HE STARTED TO HATE NERDS AND OUR iNTERESTS AND HE SAID HE WOULD BECOME THE GRAY COLOR iN OUR RAiNBOWS**," Jason added.

Everything was clear now, including the mystery behind **MR. GRAY'S** name.

Where could a guy like that hide himself?

IF WE FOUND THE STUFF HE HAD STOLEN, WE COULD SHOW THE WORLD HOW THINGS REALLY WERE AND NO ONE WOULD EVER THINK OF ME AS A FRAUD OR AN IMPOSTOR AGAIN.

"If you're wondering where he lives, I can tell you. His father was the owner of the hotel where you're staying," **JASON** said.

"So?" asked **ELLEN**.

"SO, IF HE HID THE STOLEN GOODS, THEY MUST BE SOMEWHERE IN THIS HUGE HOTEL," Jason said.

Our time had come!

My father went out to make a phone call. I was thinking about what **E.T.** had told me. What did he mean by "Look for the balance of victory?" At the hotel, I had seen a meeting hall where **Hollywood** award ceremonies were sometimes held.

145

i TOLD EVERYONE TO FOLLOW ME.

I took them to the meeting hall, hoping to amaze them.

I threw open the door.

But there was nothing to see.

I found myself in front of a stage and a hundred chairs.

"WHERE'S THE LOOT?" GEORGE asked.

Everybody was staring at me and I suddenly felt like I was a hundred pounds heavier.

On the lectern, in the middle of the stage, I saw the image of a scale.

A SCALE! Was this the "balance" that E.T. was talking about?

I touched it and the wall behind the stage opened

like a sliding door.

SUPERCOOL!!!

In front of us, there were all the stolen goods. **MR. GRAY** was sleeping in the front seat of the **DELOREAN**.

That's when I realized that the

AMERICA LOVES TALENT

cameras were filming me and my team

while we were revealing the robber.

WAKE UP!!!!!!! You can't sleep in the Delorean!

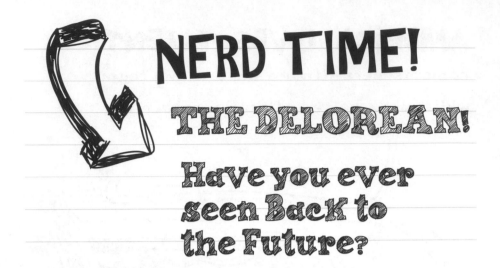

NERD TIME!

THE DELOREAN!

Have you ever seen Back to the Future?

In the Back to the Future Trilogy, the DeLorean is the time machine that the inventor "Doc" Emmett Brown (Christopher Lloyd) and his teenaged friend, Marty McFly (Michael J. Fox), use to travel through the history of their home town of Hill Valley, a fictional city in California.

In the Trilogy, the time machine was built by Doc using a normal Delorean DMC-12. But the time machine is electrical and requires a power input of 1.21 gigawatts to operate, originally provided by a plutonium-fueled nuclear reactor. In the first movie, Doc has no access to plutonium when they are stuck back in 1955, so he channels the power of a lightning bolt and sends Marty back to 1985. In Back to the Future Part II, Doc replaces the nuclear reactor with a Mr. Fusion generator that uses garbage as fuel. In Back to the Future Part III, Doc tells Marty that "the fusion device only powered the Flux Capacitor and the time circuits but the car still had an internal combustion engine that ran on gasoline."

The Delorean in Back to the Future Part II is equipped with a device that allows it to lift off from the ground and fly through the air. At the end of Part II, the device is damaged by a lightning bolt and Doc is sent back to 1885.

In the video game released for PS3 in 2011, the Delorean goes back to flying in the second of five episodes and is equipped with two new gadgets: the Automatic Retrieval System that brings the Delorean to Doc's house in the 1980s without reaching 88 mph. It goes into function after the machine hasn't been used for some time. It's a device Doc added after the events of Part III, so that Marty may be able to help him in case he couldn't get back home after a trip to the past...

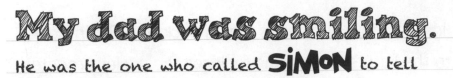

My dad was smiling.

He was the one who called **SIMON** to tell

him that I had solved the case.

BOY, WAS i HAPPY!

I had unmasked **Mr. Gray**, found

GiZMo, and **ALL THE OTHER COOL OBJECTS THAT EVERY NERD LOVES.**

I had showed the world I was a good guy.

"

SMiLE! *PHIL THE NERD* was not a

LIAR!" Rihanna said.

The cameras filmed the police waking up

MR. GRAY, AKA **RAYMOND**

MACCARTHY.

And finally, I was **Phil the Nerd**,

again!

WE WERE AT THE AIRPORT.

BiG MiND KiLL took my hand before

getting on the airplane. She whispered, so

150

the others wouldn't hear: "I LIKE YOU. YOU'RE GREAT. AS GREAT AS ONE OF THE GOONIES... PICK ONE!"

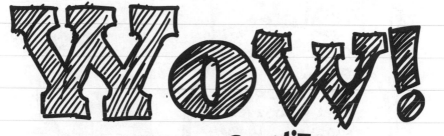

She had mentioned the **GOONIES** and I adored her!

SHE WAS A TRUE NERD and **SHE WAS SPECIAL.**

Did she want to go out with me?

I wasn't brave enough to ask if she wanted us to "be together."

Before boarding the plane, I went to the restroom and, as usual, the second I was alone, **E.T.** appeared.

"I THOUGHT YOU WERE GREAT, YOU LITTLE BRAT! You know you're growing up and, as **FANTASY BOOKS** and **MOVIES** teach us, when kids grow up their 'imaginary friends' disappear.

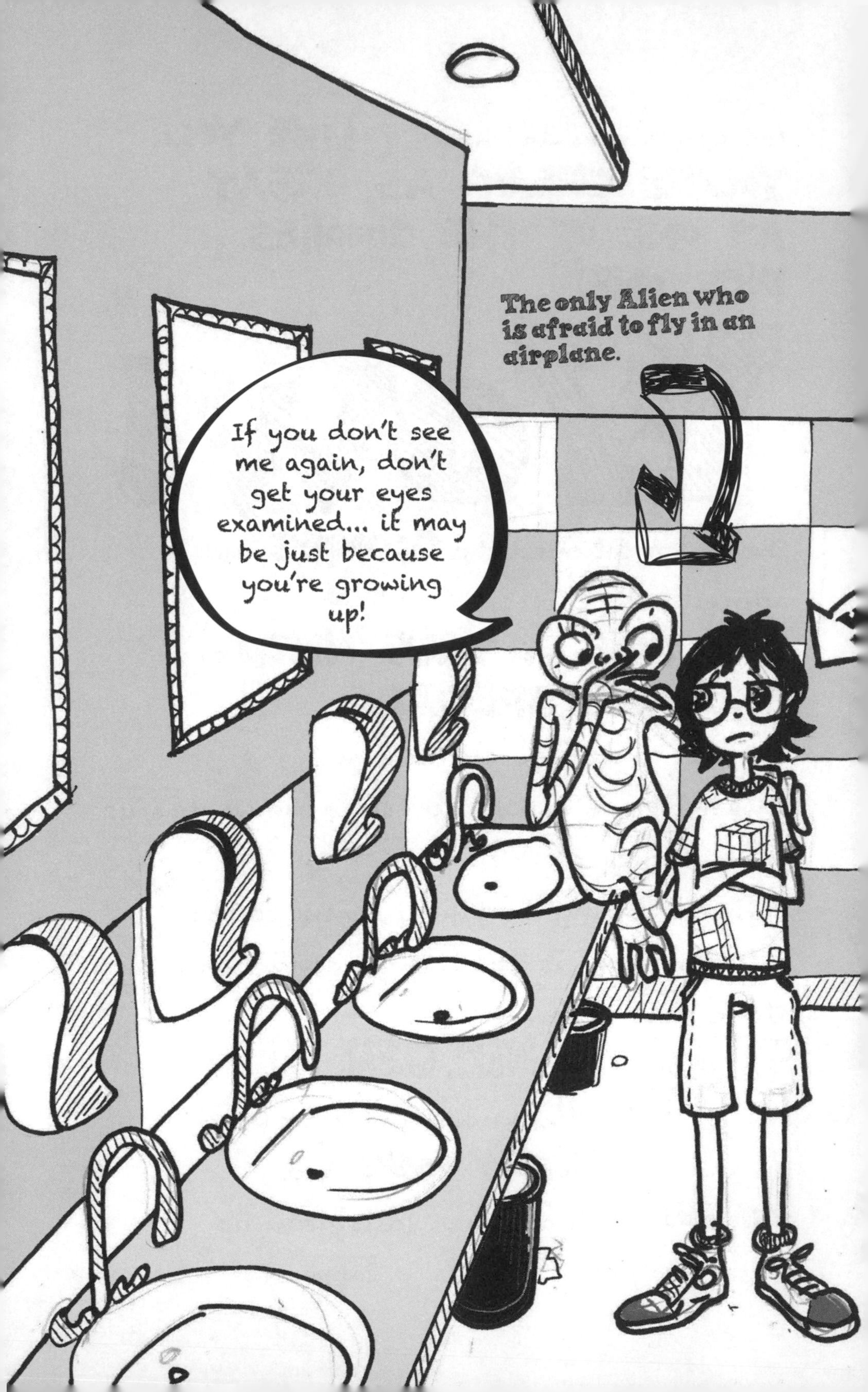
The only Alien who is afraid to fly in an airplane.
If you don't see me again, don't get your eyes examined... it may be just because you're growing up!

I was positive that my alien wasn't the real E.T., but I loved him anyway and I didn't want him to leave.

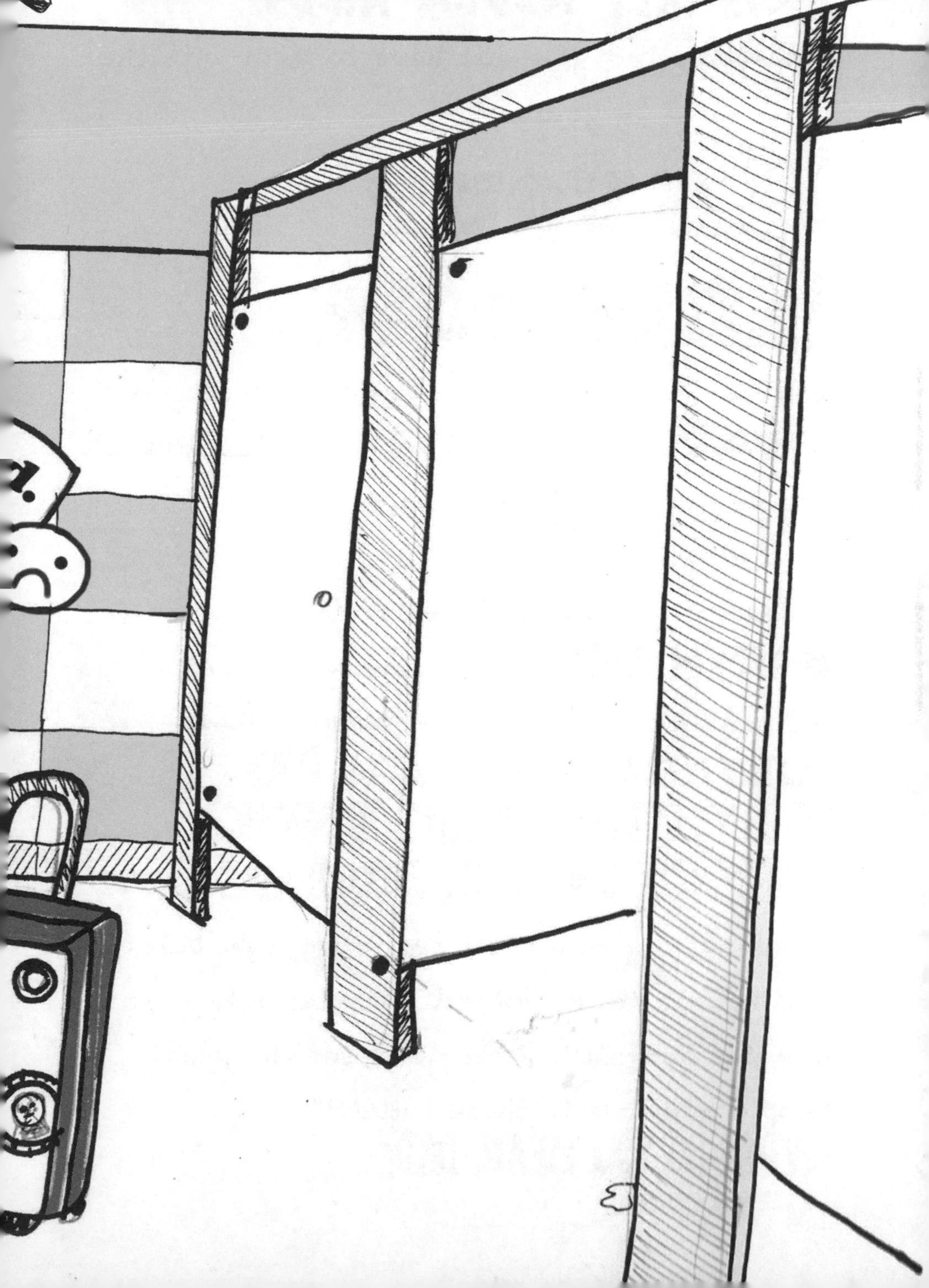

THIS MEANS WE WILL PROBABLY NEVER MEET AGAIN, and you will have to deal with the real world by yourself.

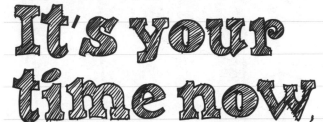

you have to live! You're not going to see me or **DARTH VADER** again because you're growing up!" the **ALIEN** said.

I was sorry I wouldn't see him or **DARTH VADER** anymore, but at the same time I was happy because **BIG MIND KILL** liked me, and **I WAS REALLY LOOKING FORWARD TO SEEING WHERE OUR LOVE STORY WOULD TAKE US.**

I got out of the airport restroom right before Dad had to go. He joined me after a few minutes and said: "You don't see the usual people anymore in these toilets!"

"WHAT DO YOU MEAN, DAD?"

"**E.T.** was in there, talking nonsense.... he was scared to fly."

"Are you telling me you've just seen **E.T.**?"

"YEAH, WHAT'S WRONG WITH THAT?"

My dad was an adult and he was still seeing the alien from **SPIELBERG'S** movie.

HOW COULD THAT BE POSSIBLE?

"Honey, come here, will you? " Mom called to Lenny.

My father quickly went over to her.

It turns out that my t-shirt designer mom had also seen an alien near the restrooms.

"He was nervous and he said there's no way he was going to get on a plane," my mom said, concerned.

Both of my parents had seen an alien despite being grown ups! **THE CRAZY EXTRATERRESTRIAL WAS REAL.**

Maybe he was not **E.T.**, maybe he was some crazy cousin of his, but he was surely part of **OUR FAMILY!**

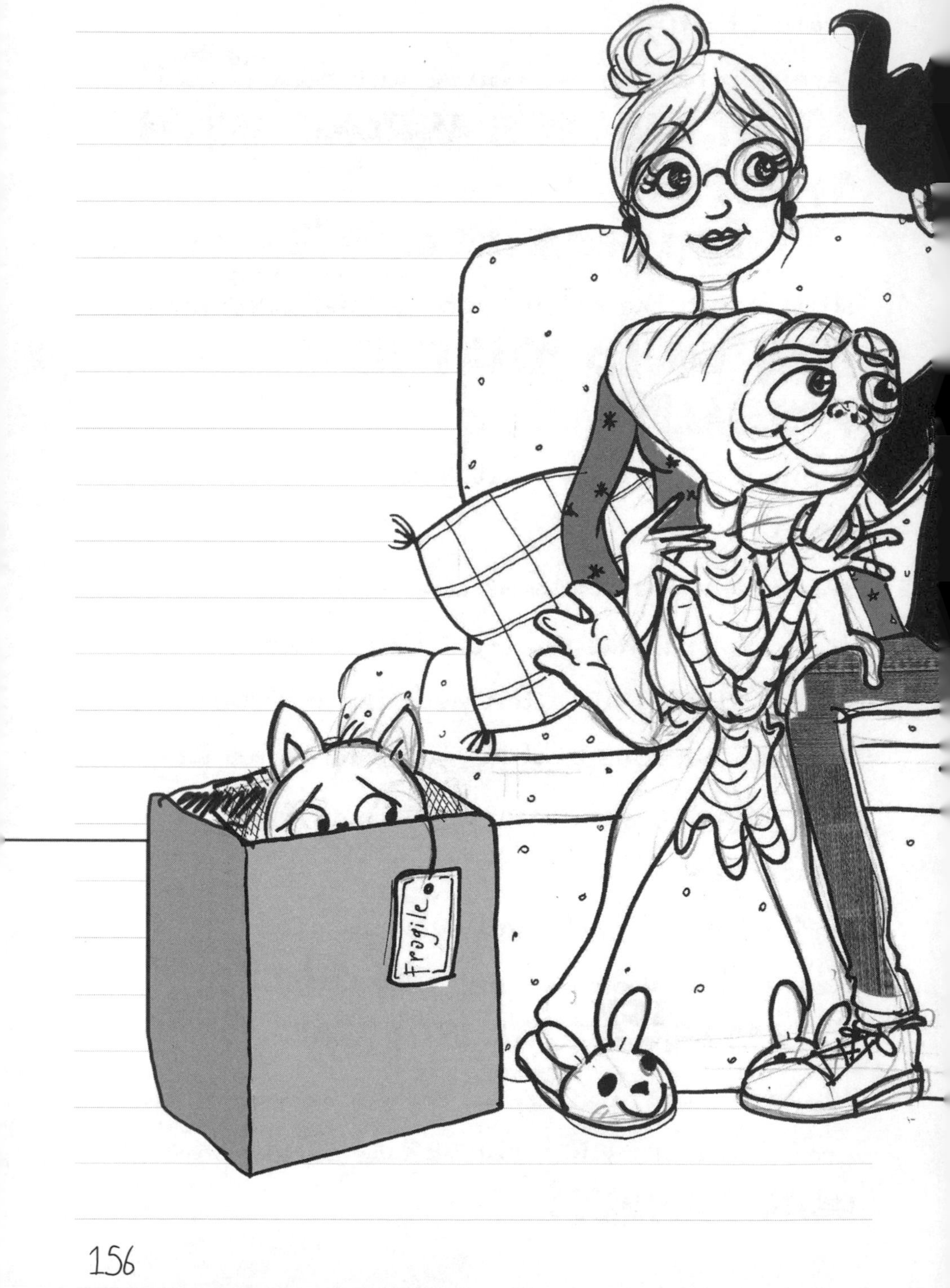
Fragile

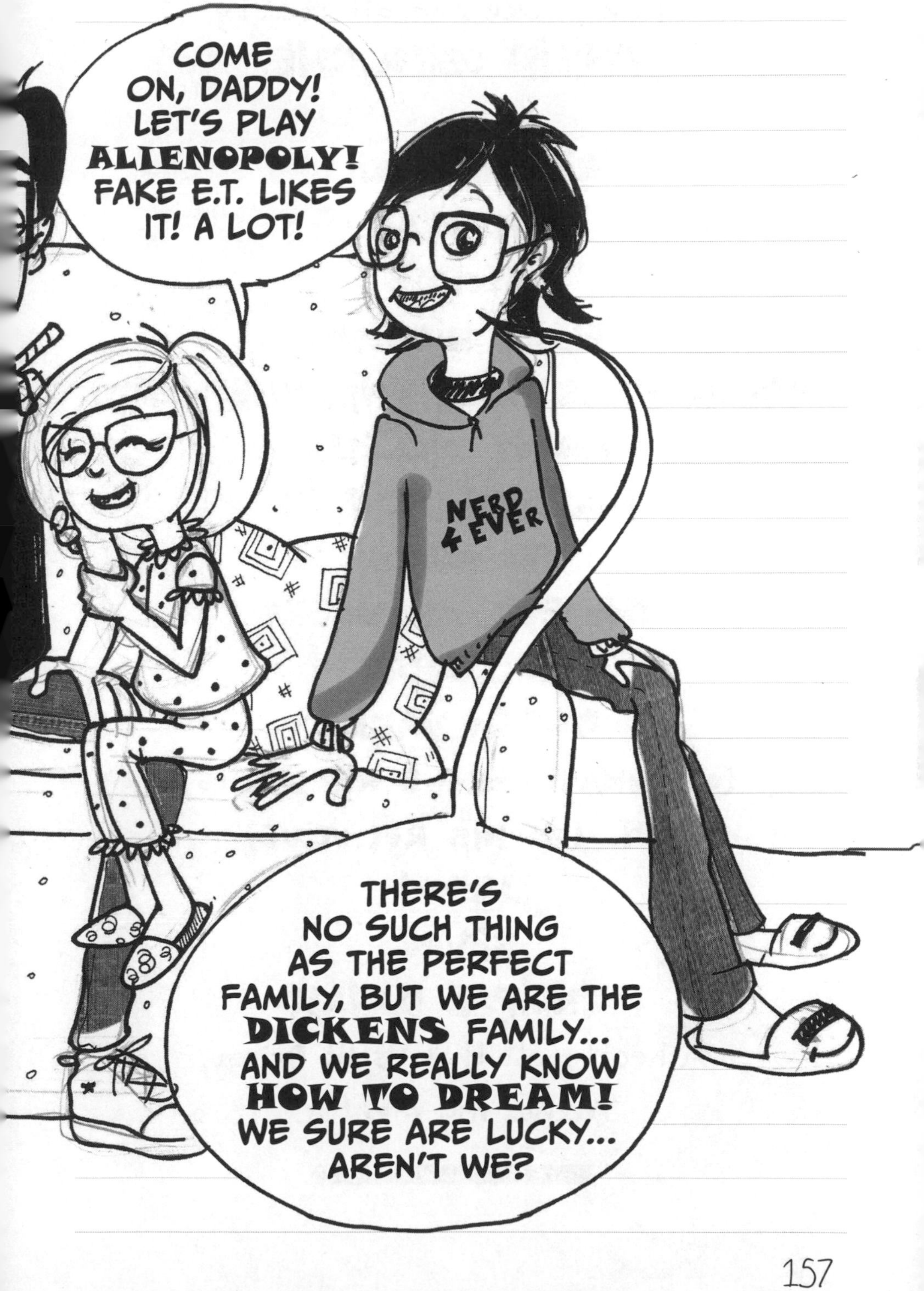
COME ON, DADDY! LET'S PLAY ALIENOPOLY! FAKE E.T. LIKES IT! A LOT!
NERD 4 EVER
THERE'S NO SUCH THING AS THE PERFECT FAMILY, BUT WE ARE THE DICKENS FAMILY... AND WE REALLY KNOW HOW TO DREAM! WE SURE ARE LUCKY... AREN'T WE?

A film written and directed by
PHILIP OSBOURNE

with

BIG MIND KILL
NICHOLAS
GEORGE
ELLEN DICKENS
PHIL DICKENS (AKA PHIL THE NERD)
LENNY DICKENS
MARILYN DICKENS
TEO MESSI
THE EVIL AVENGERS
MR. GRAY
DARTH VADER
(OR WHATEVER HE REALLY IS)
E.T. (OR HIS RELATIVE)
JASON
KEVIN
PRINCIPAL DONALD

A heart-felt thanks to Brian
Yuzna, my mentor

"BE A NERD WITH A SMILE, BE A NERD WITH LOTS OF FRIENDS AND AS STEVE JOBS, THE GREATEST OF NERDS, SAID: STAY HUNGRY. STAY FOOLISH!"

PHILIP OSBOURNE

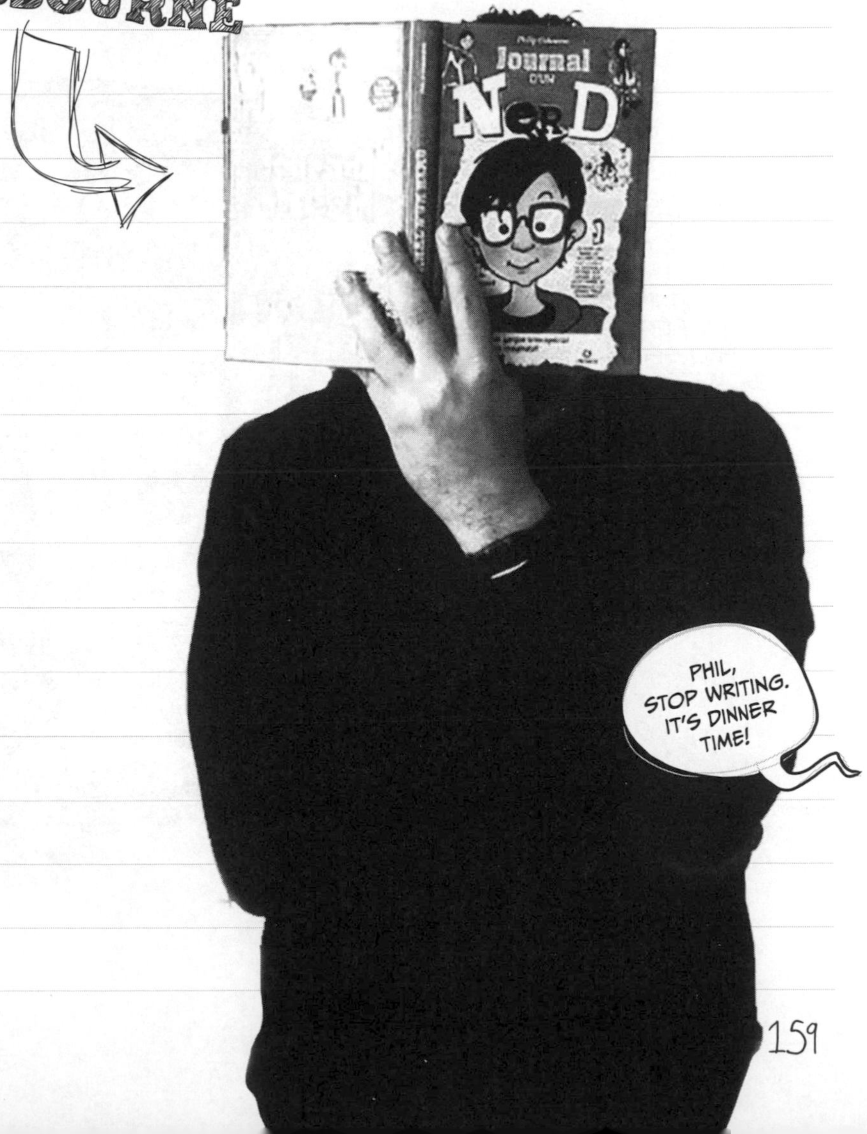
Journal
D'UN
NERD
PHIL, STOP WRITING. IT'S DINNER TIME!

PHILIP OSBOURNE

THE DIARY OF A SUPER NERD

A novel recommended for those who love fantasy and knows what it means!

PHIL BECOMES A STRANGE SUPERHERO. OUR CUTE LITTLE GENIUS TRIES TO RECREATE IN THE LABORATORY THE EXPERIMENT THAT TURNED PETER PARKER INTO SPIDER-MAN, BUT SOMETHING GOES WRONG AND PHIL TURNS INTO A SUPER LOSER...FROM GREAT POWERS COME GREAT NERDS!

...LET'S DO IT ONE MORE TIME? MAYBE THIS TIME LIKE YOU DON'T KNOW THE CAMERA IS POINTED AT YOU...